I0626029

BABY, BE MINE

By
Ginny Baird

Published by
Winter Wedding Press

Copyright 2013
Ginny Baird
Trade Paperback
ISBN 978-0-9895892-4-6

Edited by Linda Ingmanson
Cover by Dar Albert

BABY, BE MINE

TABLE OF CONTENTS

About the Author

Books by Ginny Baird

A Note from the Author

About the Author

From the time that she could talk, romance author Ginny Baird was making up stories, much to the delight—and consternation—of her family and friends. By grade school, she'd turned that inclination into a talent, whereby her teacher allowed her to write and produce plays rather than write boring book reports. Ginny continued writing throughout college, where she contributed articles to her literary campus weekly, then later pursued a career managing international projects with the US State Department.

Ginny has held an assortment of jobs, including school teacher, freelance fashion model, and greeting card writer, and has published more than ten works of fiction and optioned nine screenplays. She has additionally published short stories, nonfiction and poetry, and admits to being a true romantic at heart.

Ginny is the author of several bestselling books, including novellas in her *Holiday Brides Series*. She's a member of Romance Writers of America (RWA), the RWA Published Authors Network (PAN), and Virginia Romance Writers (VRW).

When she's not writing, Ginny enjoys cooking, biking, and spending time with her family in Tidewater, Virginia. She loves hearing from her readers and welcomes visitors to her website at http://www.ginnybairdromance.com.

Books by Ginny Baird

Holiday Brides Series
The Christmas Catch
The Holiday Bride
Mistletoe in Maine
Beach Blanket Santa
The Holiday Brides Collection
(Books 1 - 4)
Baby, Be Mine

Summer Grooms Series
Must-Have Husband
My Lucky Groom
The Wedding Wish
A Summer Grooms Selection
(Books 1 – 3)

A Haunted Holidays Special Edition
The Ghost Next Door

Other Titles
Real Romance
The Sometime Bride
Santa Fe Fortune
How to Marry a Matador
Real Romance and The Sometime Bride
(Gemini Edition)
Santa Fe Fortune and How to Marry a Matador
(Gemini Edition)

BABY, BE MINE

A Romantic Comedy Novella

Chapter One

Nikki Constantino dabbed the corner of her eye with a tissue. There was so much dust in the room, her allergies were going wild. It caked on the fake flowers in the blue vase and hung heavy in the musty air. No one must have cleaned this study in years.

The stout little man studied her kindly through horn-rimmed glasses. "I know this is hard. You and your aunt must have been close." Snow slapped the windowpanes behind him, painting icy streaks down the glass.

"Actually, I barely knew her." She sniffed, and Jack draped his arm around her. He gave her shoulder a light squeeze, the silent signal between them that everything would be all right. She didn't have to look at him to know his dark brown eyes were focused on the attorney in a way that said, *Don't sugarcoat this. Give it to us straight.*

"Nikki hasn't seen her Great-Aunt Mallory in years."

"Not since I was little. Ten, I think."

The attorney studied the papers before him and licked his plump lips. "Uh-huh," he said, thumbing through them. "Uh-huh, uh-huh, uh-huh."

Jack loudly cleared his throat. "Isn't there something you're supposed to read?"

The lawyer stared at Jack. "To Miss Constantino, yes. Frankly, not understanding your relation to the deceased, I'm not certain you should be here."

Nikki defensively took Jack's hand. "He's my best friend!"

"Friend, huh?" the other man asked, appearing amused. "I was hoping you might say fiancé."

Nikki glanced quickly at Jack, noting his neck had deepened a shade. "Why on earth would you say that?"

"Might make things less complicated."

Nikki would like to see how they could get *more* complicated. Here she sat, summoned to some tiny Midwestern town in the thick of winter, at her late great-aunt's behest. And, she hadn't a clue why. Her memories of Aunt Mallory were less than flattering and concerned an overbearing woman tottering on tiny heels. Her face was pasty pale from too much pressed powder; her lips were fire-engine red. She never seemed to get the color within the lines. And when she opened her mouth to speak, even her portly beagle, Duke, took refuge under the bed. Whether the meatloaf was overcooked or the thermostat set too low, Aunt Mallory could deliver a tongue-lashing bent in the direction of anyone careless enough to get in her way.

For the first few years after Nikki's grandma died, her mom, Emma, felt sorry for her late mother's spinster sister and invited her to join them for holidays. The invitations abruptly stopped after Mallory threatened to stuff poor Duke and pop him in the oven as a replacement for the *too dry* Thanksgiving turkey. Emma surreptitiously placed Duke with an animal rescue and sent Aunt Mallory packing. It was a transgression Aunt Mallory would never forgive. Not, apparently, until her dying day. She left her niece, Emma, nothing, and she didn't even know about Nikki's baby brother since he'd been born after she'd broken family ties. As far as Aunt Mallory was concerned, her only other remaining heir was her grand-niece, Nikki.

The attorney addressed Nikki as winds howled outside. Or maybe those were the cows crying. Could cows cry from relief, Nikki wondered? They were on Aunt Mallory's dairy farm, all fifty acres of it. Nikki certainly hoped her aunt didn't leave her *that.* She didn't know the first thing about farming. Plus, she was lactose intolerant. "Do I have your permission to proceed?"

She squeezed Jack's hand, then released it and patted his knee. She must have patted one too many times, because Jack suddenly pinned her palm in place right against his pants leg. Nikki sometimes had a nervous habit of doing something over and over, but only when she was stressed. "Whatever you have to say to me, you can say in front of Jack."

"Very well." He shuffled some papers. "I'll read what she said in her handwritten note."

"Handwritten?" Jack interceded. "Isn't a will supposed to be typed or something? Notarized?"

"She had one of those. This was written after. It supersedes the other."

Jack sat back in his chair. "I see."

She was glad he'd come along. When things crowded in on Nikki, she sometimes felt driven to react quickly, and not always in the best-thought-out ways. Like when her knee-jerk reaction was to refuse Mallory's *invite from the grave* to come here. Jack said she shouldn't look a gift horse in the mouth until she at least knew its breed. He was right, of course. There'd be no sense in refusing an inheritance sight unseen. It was just the fact it came from Aunt Mallory that made it seem unpromising. Jack was good for things like that: helping her stay charted in the right direction. She teasingly called him her compass. He didn't seem to mind the moniker. He'd had it since the tenth grade.

"*I, Mallory Gertrude Greene...*"

"Gertrude?" Jack quipped quietly beside her. She slapped his hand with her free one. He still firmly held the other. She tried to tug it away, but he resisted.

"*Being of sound mind and body,*" the attorney continued, "*do hereby bequeath my entire estate—*"

"Entire estate?" Nikki asked him. "What's that mean?"

"I'm getting to that part. *To the one relative on earth who never insulted me...*"

"That's because I was terrified," Nikki whispered to Jack.

"*My great-niece, Nicola Carina Constantino...*"

Nikki swallowed hard.

"*Under the following conditions...*"

"I didn't think the deceased could set conditions," Jack said.

"They can do anything that they want," the attorney answered. "Before I proceed, I need to read this stipulation."

"That's different from a condition?" Nikki wanted to know.

"It's a footnote." He turned the paper sideways to read something scrawled along its edge. "It says here... *Important! In order to inherit, Nicola must be over the age of twenty-five. Otherwise—*"

"Yes." Jack pumped his fist in the air, and the attorney lowered his glasses.

"This will go a lot faster without the commentary."

"Sorry." He glanced apologetically at Nikki. "It just seemed like that was a score." She'd recently turned twenty-eight, so that wasn't a problem.

The man rolled his eyes and resumed reading. *"Otherwise, the estate will be held in trust until such time Nicola reaches the age of twenty-five and is therefore is suitably mature to meet the aforesaid conditions. Assuming she does, she'll be at liberty to dispense of her inheritance as she chooses."*

Nikki's head was spinning already.

"That means you can sell the farm."

"Good." She didn't know much about real estate, but Jack was business minded. He could help her. *But wait! What if I can't sell quickly enough? What will become of the cows? I don't know a thing about milking! Yikes! What if Aunt Mallory didn't leave instructions? Will the poor cows explode? Would that make me guilty of—gasp—uddercide?*

Jack tightened his grip on her hand, sensing she was growing tense. "Breathe," he told her quietly. He demonstrated by sucking in air.

She inhaled a deep breath then let it go, feeling better. Thank goodness Jack was here. They both turned toward the attorney, who gaped at them.

"How much is it worth?" Jack asked.

The attorney raised his wrinkled brow. Nikki noticed it was flecked with age spots. "You don't know?"

She and Jack shook their heads. "This dairy has an arrangement with all the major distributors: grocery chains, restaurants... Biscuit Barrel..."

"Biscuit Barrel?" Nikki asked in surprise. She and Jack had stopped at one of those on the way here from the airport. Who knew Jack's patty melt was secretly connected?

"That sounds big," Jack said.

"It is big," the attorney answered.

"How big is *big*?" Nikki wanted to know.

"Estimated value of this farm and all your aunt's investments? Just over two million dollars."

Jack choked on the words. "Did you say two…*million*?"

"That's right. With an M."

Bright flares of light blasted before her, and Nikki wondered if she was growing faint. It was like the Fourth of July had come in December. The attorney and Jack were still talking, but she could barely hear them for all the commotion going on in her head. This was what it must feel like to win the lottery. Crazy, exhilarating… Totally surreal! She could quit her day job! Help her mom! No wait, without working, she'd probably be bored. She could become a professional playgirl, maybe. One of those jetsetters she'd heard of. Maybe even take Jack on a vacation with her. She owed him one good trip at least, after all he'd done. And to think, just last week, she'd worried over paying her heating bill.

"Nikki," Jack said, "didn't you hear any of that?"

"What?"

He clenched his jaw before speaking. "Condition one."

"No," she said breezily, mentally sketching out an itinerary. The Bahamas? Bermuda? Maybe the Caymans? Yes. Jack would probably like that. "What's condition one?"

The attorney stared at her flatly. "That you marry by Valentine's Day."

"Ma…marry?" she stammered. Impossible! Nikki didn't even have a boyfriend at the moment.

The attorney righted the hand-scrawled page. *"Tie the knot. Get hitched. Ball and chain. Hook, line, and sinker, yes."*

"She wrote that?" Jack asked in shock.

"Every word, including that next thing about the baby."

"Baby?" Nikki squeaked. Now she was certain she would faint.

The attorney shook out the page and flipped it over. "That's condition two."

"Your Aunt Mallory apparently thought she could dictate not just your marriage but your entire life," Jack said, growing indignant.

"She does give you an extra year for the child. To produce one, I mean."

"Great!" Nikki chirped cheerily. "Mallory's just the one to give family advice!"

"Maybe she wants you to have what she didn't," the attorney noted astutely.

"What makes you say that?" Jack asked.

"It's in her PS here. And this is to Nicola. *PS: Just in case you're wondering why I'm doing this, dear child, it's for your own good. Life is too short to die embittered and alone. It might take a while, but you'll understand this yourself one day. You'll be thanking me until the cows come home."*

"Until the cows come home?" Nikki asked weakly.

"It's an expression," the lawyer said.

Jack translated. "For a really long time."

"Huh?"

"Cows are very slow creatures," the lawyer explained. "I think she meant forever."

"Oh."

"This is crazy," Jack said to the lawyer. "You know it is."

He held up his hands. "I didn't make the rules here. I'm just the referee."

The fog in Nikki's brain lifted. "Can we contest it?"

"Sure you can." He sat back in his chair and crossed his arms. "Just as long as you think you can move things through the courts before that February fourteenth deadline."

"But that's less than eight weeks away!"

"What if we can't?" Jack asked.

"It's a risk. You'll have to prove that Mallory was unstable when she wrote this. I mean, more so than in her previous days. You'll also have to find a judge who will hear your case. We're not talking weeks now. We're talking months. Years, more than likely. But you're young. You've got plenty of time."

Yeah, maybe she did, but her mother didn't. Nikki would have to talk to Jack about that. Talk to him seriously. "What becomes of the farm in that case?"

"It gets stuck in probate."

"And the cows?"

The attorney stroked his chin. "The people your aunt hired to work this farm can continue for a while but not indefinitely. Certainly not without being paid. Mallory left behind enough money to keep them on through the end of February. At that point, I think she assumed you'd either take over running the business or sell it off."

Nikki's voice rose in panic. "But I don't *own* the business."

"You will by February fourteenth—if you marry."

Jack finally released her hand and leaned forward on his elbows. "And if she doesn't?"

"Everything will be liquidated and absorbed by the state."

"What do you mean liquidated?" Nikki asked. "They won't hurt the cows?"

"I can't say what will become of the cows. Perhaps another dairy will take them, or they'll be farmed out to different ones. There are other options too. But you may not want to hear about them."

Nikki gasped. She *was* about to become responsible for uddercide. How horrifying!

"Holy cow," Jack said. "This is a mess."

The attorney handed Nikki a weighty portfolio. "I'd encourage you not to make any rash decisions until you've read this. In spite of what you think of it, your Aunt Mallory's bequest to you was really quite generous."

Nikki nodded numbly, seeming to have lost all sense of time. "What day is it?"

"December twenty-fifth," Jack said.

The attorney dismissed them with a smile. "Merry Christmas."

Jack stopped Nikki as she was about to lay her hand on the latch that opened the barn door. "Are you sure you want to do this?"

Winds whistled around them, riffling through her layered brown hair. It fell in waves past her shoulders above her puffy white coat and was now dotted with flakes from the driving snow. She met Jack's gaze with pretty blue eyes that had his caused his heart to skip a beat ever since high school. Not that she'd ever know he still felt that way. That was Jack's little secret.

"Positive," she told him. "One hundred percent." But when she shoved at the latch, it appeared to be frozen.

Jack had to muscle in beside her to get it unstuck. "Here, let me."

Her hand-knit mittens with the funky patterned stitch slid out of the way just as loud mooing erupted. Nikki jumped back with a start. "What was that?"

"Your cow babies," Jack said with a smile. "To be."

Nikki dusted the snow from her hair and shoulders, then stepped past him when he opened the door. "Ew!" She covered her mouth against the stench. "Really!"

"They've got to go somewhere," he told her, jimmying the door shut.

She stared up and down rows of stalls as huge brown eyes turned in her direction. "Mooo!" one cow bellowed. Nikki surveyed a large one that appeared to be nearly twice the size of the others. "Jack, look!" She pointed to a metal plaque that hung above the cow's head. "Mallory named them."

Jack read the lettering. This one had been named *Mama*. "I think she forgot the *Big* in front of that."

Mama craned her neck forward, and Nikki tentatively patted her head.

Jack spoke from behind her. "Hey there, Ma. How's it going?"

"Stop it," Nikki scolded. "You're making fun of her." The cow met her gaze in agreement and tried to nuzzle closer, but a stall crossbar stopped her. Nikki studied the host of equipment protruding from the far wall. "That's ghastly. Do they hook her up to that?"

"I'm guessing they do."

Nikki frowned. "Doesn't seem like a very good life."

"Maybe it's all she knows?" He gave the cow a pat, and they kept walking. Jack was impressed by the size of the operation. From the outside of the barn, he'd had no idea. No wonder Nikki's aunt raked in a fortune in Cheez Whiz. They passed stall after stall, each of them labeled with an individual name.

Nikki paused before one, her jaw dropping. "She didn't."

Jack surveyed the name plaque with amusement. "Maybe she meant it as a compliment?" He reached toward the cow. "Here, Nikki, Nikk… Nikk—"

Nikki slapped his hand away. "Very funny." But her lips twisted up slightly at the corners, and Jack knew she saw the humor in the situation as well.

"Could have been worse," he said, glancing back at Mama.

Nikki started to say something smart, but then her face fell in sadness. "Jack," she said, slowly meeting his eyes. "They *will* be okay? All of them?"

Hoo boy, he'd known this was a bad idea from the moment she suggested it. The last thing someone as caring as Nikki needed to do was go involving her emotions in what was already primed to be a highly charged situation. "I'm sure your aunt wouldn't really have left them without some sort of plan."

Big Mama mooed.

"She's right," Nikki said. "You didn't know her."

She set her chin and glanced around the crowded barn.

"You seen enough?"

Nikki paused a long while before answering. Finally, she said, "We've got to find a way to fix this, Jack. A way to make it work for everyone."

"I know you have a soft spot for animals, Nikki, but—"

"For *everyone*, Jack. Not just them."

She dove into his soul with a stare, and Jack knew that whatever was coming next was serious. "I haven't told you about my mom. But I will."

"When?"

"Tonight, when we get back to our motel. But first…" She wiped back a tear with her mitten. "I need to get out of here."

Nikki sat across from Jack as he munched on his Philly cheese steak sandwich. He'd insisted they grab a bite before heading back to their motel, and he'd been right. They'd done delivery pizza the night before and had spent half an hour arguing over ingredients. Jack took another bite, and melted cheese oozed out the side of his sub.

Nikki set down her salad fork. "I wish you hadn't done that."

Jack stared at her with utmost innocence. "What?"

"Ordered *that*."

"Hey, look." Jack wiped his mouth with a napkin. "Just because you've gone all vegan on me doesn't mean I can't enjoy a bit of beef."

"Bad time to order cow, Jack. Not to mention provolone."

"Well, Ms. Cream-of-Mushroom-Soup—but oh! Can you hold the cream? What would you have suggested instead?"

Nikki frowned at the nasty cup of soup she'd pushed aside. She really should have known better at a place called the Royal Corral. When she made her request, the server looked at her like she'd arrived from

Mars. Everything on the menu involved either meat or dairy, except for the meager side salad, which Nikki eagerly dug into now. "I'm just saying you could have showed a bit of sensitivity."

"Sorry." Jack picked his sandwich back up. "My sensitivity doesn't extend all the way down to my stomach."

They finished their food in silence, and Jack could tell Nikki was growing grumpy, like she did when her blood sugar got low. Maybe they could find something on the dessert menu to perk her up, assuming the pie a la mode could be served without the ice cream. "Hey, look," he told her. "It's really not that bad. It's not like the world's coming to an end or anything like that."

"Tell that to Big Mama."

"We really shouldn't have gone in that barn."

"Of course we should have." Her pretty blue eyes flashed with determination. "I needed to see for myself what I was getting into."

"Or out of, Nikki. There's still time to get out of it." She stared at him. "Your aunt's ridiculous condition, I mean."

"Conditions," she corrected. "With an S."

"Yeah, both of them. I can call my cousin Dave. He's a lawyer. Maybe he knows someone up here."

"I appreciate what you're trying to do, but—"

"But what?"

She inhaled deeply, then let it out. "I could really use that money, Jack."

"Yeah." He laughed lightly. "We could all use a couple of million. But not all of us are willing to sell ourselves for it."

"You make it sound so cold."

"Blame Mallory, not me." He studied her a beat, noting her expression had grown cloudy. "Is there something else going on that I don't know about?"

"My mom's not getting any better."

"That neck thing?"

"Her slipped disk, yeah."

"I thought she was going to have surgery?"

Nikki looked at him sadly. "She can't afford it."

"What about the diner? Don't they provide insurance?"

"It's a crappy plan, barely covers half the cost." Her brow creased with worry. "It hurts her every day to go to work. Even getting up in the morning is painful."

"She said that?"

"She didn't have to. I've seen how she moves."

"Well, maybe she can get a loan, talk to the doctors? Hospitals sometimes have repayment plans."

"We've looked into that. I even offered to help."

Jack understood that was generous, but he also knew Nikki didn't make a lot of money herself on her department store tailor's salary.

"But she's too proud. She'd never take me up on it, knowing I barely scrape by myself. Besides, she says if I'm going to help anyone out, it should be Tony."

"Tony?"

"He graduates high school this year, and really has his heart set on going to college."

"That's expensive these days."

"Way costly. Even in state."

"What about scholarships? He's a good student, right?"

"State assistance was cut back with the recent budget cuts. He says he may have to put off going. Work a few years first."

Jack studied her with sympathy. "Sounds rough."

"Some days Ma can't even make it in to work. They dock her pay in that case. And she's got a mortgage to meet and bills to pay for Tony."

Jack stared at her with incredulity. "Just what are you saying? That you're considering meeting your Aunt Mallory's conditions?"

"Maybe it won't be so bad? In the short term."

He leaned forward and touched her arm. "But in the long term? Over time?"

"I'm not saying it has to last forever. Me and the prospective"—she appeared to nearly choke on the word—"*groom* can cut a deal."

Jack massaged his brow. "Who are you planning to marry, Nikki? You're not even seeing Dean anymore."

"That's true." She licked her lips and sat up a little straighter. "But I'll find someone, don't you think? I'm not such a bad a catch. Especially not for half a million dollars."

"I thought it was two?"

"That's the amount I'm willing to share with someone who'll go through with it. I guess if they insist, I could negotiate up to half the total."

"Now you're talking crazy."

"No, I'm being reasonable." And when she said it, for a lunatic instant, it looked like she believed it.

"So you're going to go out there and find someone to marry. Just like that! By February fourteenth."

"Yes."

"Who?"

"I don't know. I guess I'd better start looking."

Although he suspected the outcome, Jack decided to chance it anyway. "You could always marry me…?"

"Oh, Jack, please be serious!"

He affected a chuckle to make it seem like he'd been kidding. "Well, someone's got to lighten the mood around here."

"Yeah, right. You're a very funny guy. But most importantly, you're my best friend. Which is why you've got to help me."

Jack adored Nikki, would move heaven and earth for her. But help her find another man to marry? He wasn't sure he could do that.

"Come on, Jack, *puleeze?*" She batted those eyes, and Jack knew he was a goner. He'd never been able to refuse Nikki anything in his entire life. And now his life, and all the secret hopes and dreams he'd harbored, were about to be harpooned by her ludicrous request. "I've always wanted a baby."

"There are places you can go for that without signing the rest of your life away."

"It's not the rest of my life. I don't even have to stay married. Just long enough to get pregnant."

Jack willed his mind not to go there. There was nothing worse than thinking of Nikki with another guy. When she was with a boyfriend, it was easy enough for him to push those thoughts away completely. It was when she was *between them* that Jack's hopes became renewed. Time and time again. When would he ever learn? Hadn't Nikki made things clear enough the night of their senior prom?

She appeared to be thinking, those mental wheels turning in some sort of diabolical plan. When she set her gaze back on his, she seemed buoyed, as if she'd convinced herself this entire wacky scheme could work.

"We'll have the kid call you Uncle Jack," she continued brightly. "In the end, you'll probably be closer to him than his own dad. It's not like *Dad* will be much in the picture. That will be part of the deal."

Jack felt the burn in his eyes but smiled tightly to disguise his feelings. "What if *Dad* doesn't agree?"

She brushed aside his concerns with a wave of her hand. "Aren't you the one who's fond of saying there's always a way to work things out?"

Now she was twisting his words to serve them back at him. "Nikki—"

"Don't *Nikki* me. You know we can do this, you and me. If anyone can pull it off, we can." She reached across the table to take his hands. "Please tell me you'll help. Help Ma. Help Tony, and…" She hesitated, then said with a desperate look, "Big Mama."

Jack pursed his lips, knowing there was no way he could do it. But in a stronger sense, he knew he couldn't deny helping the one person on earth he loved. Nikki'd had his heart forever, and now—without even being aware—she was going to stomp all over it. And Jack was going to help her, damn it. Help her because he understood that if he couldn't be hers, he'd better damn well ensure that the guy who was deserved her. For Nikki wasn't just beautiful. She was smart and funny, and such great company to be around. The fact was, he'd rather hang out with her than any of his buddies. She was way more entertaining and very easy to be with. Nikki had that eclectic blend of streetwise and sophisticated, with her own unique quirkiness mixed in. And Jack found that headily intoxicating. Now he was about to help someone else get drunk on her. Once they did, and discovered what is was like living with her day after day, Jack was certain no man in his right mind would be willing to give up Nikki. Worst-case scenario, she might even start falling for him... This was turning out to be a very un-merry Christmas for sure.

Jack fought the lump in his throat and squeezed Nikki's hands. "What are best friends for?"

Chapter Two

Nikki sat cross-legged on one double bed while Jack propped himself up against some pillows on the other. They'd been too cheap to get separate rooms. Besides, what did she have to worry about with Jack? Nikki reached into her large corduroy bag and withdrew Jack's present. She'd nearly forgotten what day it was until the attorney reminded them. Christmas. Who would have thought she'd be spending it in some budget motel with Jack?

"Here," she said, handing him the gift. "I got you something."

He looked up from where he'd been busily typing a message into his smartphone. "You what?" he asked, setting his phone on the nightstand.

"For Christmas, you big monkey. Go on," she urged. "Take it."

He reached across the narrow space between them and accepted the package, visibly touched. "Geez, Nikki. You didn't have to. Especially with this sudden trip… How did you…?"

"Got it a while ago. On sale," she lied. The truth was this holiday gesture had cost her a fortune. Nearly a week's wages, in fact. But if anyone deserved it, Jack did. Nobody had stood by her the way Jack had, not even any of her girlfriends over the years.

He tore back the wrapping and extracted the gift CD. Then his face fell.

"What's wrong?" she asked. "Don't tell me you already have it?" It was a new Christmas album release of Jack's favorite jazz artist. It had only been available since Thanksgiving.

"I love it." He met her eyes, and his own registered sadness. "It's the best. You're the best. The only thing is…" He hesitated a moment, holding the CD in his hands. "I didn't bring your present with me."

"Is that all?" she asked, relieved. "Gosh, Jack, you had me worried there I'd really flubbed something up."

"You never mess things up," he told her, his fingers apparently skimming the tickets taped to the back of the case. He flipped it over in awe. "You didn't." Though their surroundings were dreary, Jack's smile lit up the whole shabby room. Nikki couldn't help but think how good-looking he was. Tall, dark, and handsome, and a totally great guy too. What was wrong with the women out there?

He leapt off his bed to give her a hug. "I can't believe you did this! This is amazing, Nikki. *You're* amazing. Thanks so much."

She hugged him back, laughing. "Hey, it's only tickets and not a backstage pass."

"Doesn't matter." He settled down on the bed beside her, studying the tickets like they were some sort of holy grail. "I see you got me two," he said, fanning them in the air.

"I was hoping you might get lucky."

"Thanks for your vote of confidence."

"No, seriously. How long has it been?"

"Since?"

"Don't play cute with me. I know you've been seeing Veronica."

"Well, maybe it's none of your business."

"You know all of mine."

"That's because you've got a great big blabbermouth."

"I do not!"

"Um-hmm," he said smugly. "But, no worries. Your secrets are safe with me. All of them."

She nabbed a pillow and bopped him over the head.

"Ow! What was that for?"

"For being such a smartie. And for forgetting my gift!"

He grabbed a pillow and slammed her back, whacking her across the shoulder. "And that's for not giving me the benefit of the doubt!"

"Hey!" She hit him again, harder this time, clean across the chest, then fell back with a giggle.

"Oh no, you don't..." he said, clobbering her again.

She raised her eyebrows, and he tackled her by the shoulders, tumbling forward. Nikki stopped laughing as he lay on top of her on the bed, his torso pinning hers to the mattress. She could feel the solidity of his frame, the lean muscles in his thighs and chest, the power of his masculinity above her. Jack looked down at her with deep brown eyes, and she could swear she could hear every measure of his breathing. Or maybe it was her own breath that was coming out in rapid puffs as her heart hammered hard between them. "Nikki, I..."

She felt fire in her cheeks as her heart careened wildly out of control. "Jack... What are you doing?"

He blinked hard, then pushed back, rolling off her and onto the mattress. She hoped he would say something, but even she couldn't explain what had just happened. It was as if in that split-second he'd gone from being just Jack to some sexy, desirable...

The pillow crashed down on her crown with a thwunk! "*That*," he teased, "is a lesson in what happens when you tempt fate."

Nikki grabbed another pillow away from him before he could nail her again. "Oh, so you're *fate* now?" she asked, clutching the pillow against her.

Jack rolled onto his side and stared at her, dark eyes dancing. "One day, some woman will call me her destiny."

Nikki's breath caught in her throat, because she knew that was true. Jack wouldn't be single forever. Someone out there was bound to snap him up, and then what would become of their friendship? Another woman might not be as understanding as Jack had been of Nikki having boyfriends. "I'm sure that's true."

His brow rose in amusement. "What? No snarky comebacks? No contest?"

But Nikki didn't want to banter anymore with Jack, not even if it was play arguing. She was having a difficult enough time getting the feel of his rock-hard body out of her mind. She handed him the pillow she'd been holding and sat up. "I'm going to grab a shower."

He appraised her as if he was trying to discern whether something was wrong. "All right."

"And when I'm done, we need to talk about wardrobe for the funeral tomorrow."

"I thought we were talking about finding the guy you're going to marry?" he called after her as she strode toward the bathroom.

"That too!" she answered, shutting the bathroom door. Then she ran the shower water until it came out icy cold and stepped inside.

Nikki stood beside Jack under the green canvas tent. The sky beyond them was gray, with big, dark clouds hovering above. The snow had stopped, but that didn't take the edge off the bitter winds. Nikki gathered her arms around her, gripping her elbows for warmth. She and Jack hadn't discussed wardrobe last night. In fact, they hadn't discussed anything at all. When she'd emerged from the bathroom, he'd fallen dead asleep. On her bed no less. She'd had to take the other one. She cast a furtive glance his way, noting he'd dressed in a dark suit and tie, his charcoal-colored overcoat appropriately morose. She, on the other hand, wore white. Not that she could help the color of her down jacket, or the fact that her handmade scarf, hat, and mittens were brightly patterned in oranges and blues. Their base color was neutral, though: a soft beige shade, somewhere between off-white and tan. While her sweater was baby blue, her skirt, tights, and boots were jet black. So at least she was dressed right from the waist down.

Jack elbowed her, and she realized the minister had just finished his prayer. She added her "*Amen*" just in time, so as not to sound out of step with the others. Not that there were many others present. There was the attorney from yesterday, somebody from the bank, she had learned, plus some sort of investment portfolio manager. Money people, every last one. Did her Aunt Mallory leave no personal connections behind? As the minister said his final words, she viewed the urn before them that contained Aunt Mallory's ashes. It was simple but tasteful in marbled black. Nikki had taken care to lay some flowers before it. She and Jack picked them up at a small grocery store on the way over. Now she was glad they had. They were the only things that

leant a bit of warmth to this perfunctory service.
Though she hadn't seen her in years, and really hadn't
liked her when she'd known her, Nikki couldn't help
but feel sad for her late great-aunt. What a depressing
way to die. Truly all alone.

The minister finished up, and she thanked him for
his time. Jack slipped him some cash, and Nikki was
glad he'd thought of it. Compensating the clergy hadn't
been on her mind. There'd been so much to do and
arrange during their hurry to get here. She'd only
received the call on Christmas Eve, and the interment
was to occur just two days later. If she could get there
in time, the attorney said he'd prefer to read Aunt
Mallory's will prior to the funeral. He had other
commitments afterward that couldn't be rearranged.
Nikki had agreed to fly right up and meet with him the
next day. The whole thing had taken her by surprise,
and she was eager to get things done with. She never
could have guessed the reading of the will would leave
her with a whole new problem.

After they said their good-byes to the others, Jack
turned to her.

"You want to stay until it's finished?"

Nikki eyed the two grave workers appointed by the
cemetery to lower the urn in the ground. She felt an
unexpected lump in her throat, thinking about how lost
and lonely her Aunt Mallory must have felt. She had to
have been pretty desperate to write that kind of crazy
will. Desperate enough to want to ensure that her grand-
niece wouldn't suffer the same fate. "Yeah," she said
softly. "I think we'd better."

Jack nodded and stood by her, not bothering to
offer further condolences or make unnecessary small
talk. He knew her well enough to read her mood and

could likely see she wasn't interested in conversation. Just by being there he said a lot. And, at that precise heartbreaking moment, that was all Nikki needed to hear.

Later, Jack steered their rental car toward the airport as Nikki stared out the window. She'd been really down since the funeral and had barely spoken during the time they'd packed up and checked out of their motel. "It was good of you to want to stay," he told her. "Until the end, I mean."

"It seemed like the right thing to do."

"Yeah." After a beat, he asked, "You doing okay?"

"I'll probably feel better once we're on the plane."

"And you order a scotch and soda?" Jack knew Nikki didn't drink much and rarely imbibed hard liquor. Except when circumstances were extreme. This seemed like one of those times.

She laughed lightly, her dark mood brightening. "You really do know me."

"I've had a few years on the job," he quipped back.

"Oh, so I'm *work* now, am I?"

His lips twitched in a smile. "You can be."

"Fine, you can think that." She adjusted her shoulder harness and repositioned herself in her seat. "Just don't tell that to Dean."

"Dean?" He was Nikki's last boyfriend. They'd broken up eight months ago. "What's he got to do with anything?"

"That's where we're starting. My most recent mistake makes the most sense."

He stared at her, then set his gaze back on the road. "I wish you could hear yourself talking."

"I am hearing myself, and I think I'm making perfect sense. Dean's the logical choice. He's my most recent…involvement. He's smart, hot, and just a little bit sexy."

Jack blinked.

"Okay. Sexy enough. I could have his baby, I think."

He couldn't believe she was actually going to do this. Cave to her aunt's ridiculous request. "So, you're going to what? Just walk right up and ask him?"

"No. I'm going to suggest we meet in the park."

He knew that Nikki and Dean had met in Boston Common. She'd been pet sitting for a neighbor, and he'd been out walking his dog. Their leashes had gotten tangled just like in some silly romantic comedy. "You're going to get nostalgia working for you?"

"That and a little bit of cash. I'll explain the whole thing to him."

"But Dean doesn't need the money. He does well enough in business."

"Everybody can use an extra million."

Yeah, even me. Although, if Jack were to marry Nikki, it certainly wouldn't be for the money. He glanced her way, spying her jaw set in that determined fashion that said she believed she'd come up with a great idea and was prepared to act on it.

"It won't be so bad," she told him. "I actually *liked* Dean."

"Yeah, but like and love are two separate things."

"Yes, like I *love* my mother and my baby brother, and have developed a deep…affection for a barn full of cows, including Big Mama."

"You're determined to do this, aren't you? What if Dean doesn't work out?"

"Gosh, Jack." She sounded mildly offended. "It's not like I don't have options."

He knew that much was true. If "options" was a code word for exes, Nikki had plenty.

"If Dean's not interested, I'll talk to Jeremy. And then Gordon."

"Kurt?

"Even Peter."

"Geez, Nikki. Are you sure about this?"

"In the past twenty-four hours, I've thought a lot about it. Yes. Tons of places in the world have arranged marriages. People marry for lots of reasons, including benefiting their families. In a way, it's nothing new. I'll just be upholding a centuries-old tradition that still plays out in many parts of the planet today."

"But this is *America*. The US of A."

"That means I get to make my own choices, doesn't it? Do whatever I decide is right for me?"

If only he could believe it *was* right. But everything about this whole twisted scheme screamed wrong, wrong, *wrong*! "I thought the deal was you were only getting married for a year. Just long enough conceive."

"Maybe we'll grow to love each other," she said a bit wistfully.

He stared at her in disbelief.

"Really! It happens all the time."

"Most often, I've seen it happen the other way. People start out head-over—"

"Will you stop being such a pessimist, for just one second? I mean, once we have a child between us, it only makes sense to give it a go."

Jack massaged his forehead with one hand while keeping the other firmly on the wheel. Maybe he was the one who needed a scotch and soda. Heavy on the scotch. *Better make mine a double.*

Chapter Three

A few days later, Jack huddled under an umbrella and sipped from his coffee. Tiny icicles rained down from the sky in spiky jabs, prickling his neck and bare knuckles. He'd been in such a rush to get here, he'd forgotten to bring his leather gloves. She'd only given him an hour's notice about the meeting. That was just like Nikki. She was impetuous and emotional, and so last minute. Undeniably, he found those things charming. But Jack also knew Nikki well enough to guess she wanted to barrel through this first attempt before she lost her nerve. Jack clutched his paper cup as she approached. She wore a luminous raincoat that matched the bright red polka dots on her umbrella. Waves of luscious brown hair spilled out from beneath her knit cap as her blue eyes sparkled. She strode past him and whispered, "Wish me luck…"

"Luck!" he called after her, but he didn't mean it. The last thing he wanted was for Nikki to go marrying another guy. At the far end of the park, he spied Dean standing by a hedge abutting the lake, his tall, lean form framed by Boston's highest buildings. They stood like gloomy towers in the fog, but nothing could feel more dismal than the ache in Jack's heart. He'd scarcely slept last night, tossing and turning over this whole ordeal. In the end, he'd decided the best thing he could do was play along. Nikki was headstrong enough to forge her own path, and any resistance she encountered would only lend that much more zeal to her quest. If Jack took it easy—even acted supportive—Nikki was sure to see the error of her ways.

Dean spotted Nikki, and his expression brightened. They embraced briefly, umbrellas tilting backward as an icy stream of rain shimmied down between them. Both laughed and wiped their clothing, appearing to chat easily over small talk. He was probably asking her how she'd been, and she was likely suggesting he help her make a baby. Jack felt his neck flash hot and his temples pound at that last thought. It was hard to forget what had transpired in their motel room when he and Nikki had been kidding around. From one moment to the next, they'd morphed from long-time friends into potential lovers. It had lasted only a second, but Jack had felt that fire down to his very core. He wondered if Nikki had sensed it too.

Suddenly, Dean seemed taken aback. He thrust his hands to the side, setting his umbrella askew and letting his head get drenched in the process. He didn't seem to notice the rain as he stared agape at Nikki. Then he began speaking rapidly, righting his umbrella in one hand, then pulling something from his coat pocket with the other. It was a wallet. He flipped it open. *What on earth? Did she require identification? Or a sperm count?*

Nikki took the billfold and studied something inside it, her face falling. *I see,* she appeared to be telling him. *Who knew?* Then she flipped the thing shut with a shrug.

Dean tucked the wallet in his pocket and shook his head. The next thing Jack knew, Dean was shaking his finger at Nikki. Scolding her, he supposed, for the very idea as she backed away. Nikki cast a tight grin in Jack's direction, knowing he was waiting. Dean wheeled toward him. *Wait a minute,* he seemed to think. *Jack's been watching?* Dean's voice was harsh, cracking in the morning air as she retreated quickly toward Jack and he barked after her, "That's rich, Nikki! Just rich!" He shook the heavy moisture from his umbrella, then straightened it and strode away. Nikki scurried toward Jack.

"Didn't go so well, I take it?"

She was out of breath, little puffs of air appearing between hot-pink lips. "It was awful. *He* was awful. And to think I might have married him!"

"Hmm, yes."

"After all this time, I thought he still might care."

"You were together three years."

"That's what I told him. Exactly."

"What was in the wallet?"

"A picture of Mary Ann, and—get this—her three kids!"

"Who's Mary Ann?"

"His wife!"

"Guess you're a little late."

"Here's the horrible thing. Dean used to say he'd never have kids."

"Then, why did you—?"

"He said not at least until he turned thirty. Which would have been perfect, since he's twenty-nine and a half."

She gazed at him, desperation in her eyes. "And now he's gone and gotten the package deal!"

"Well, you *have* been apart a while."

"Eight months? That's more than a kid a quarter!"

"But they're not *his*—biologically, I mean. Right?"

"Mary Ann's his old college girlfriend. They broke up after school, and she married someone else."

"It apparently didn't last."

"She told Dean she'd never forgotten him. That he was the only guy she'd ever loved. I guess he decided the feeling was mutual."

"Ouch. He said that?"

"Said what?"

"That Mary Ann was the only woman he'd ever loved?"

"Thanks for rubbing it in, Jack. I didn't even think about it that way."

The wind picked up, rustling her raincoat and billowing their umbrellas.

"I'm sorry, Nikki. Really, I am." In a strange sort of way, he saw it was true. He hated seeing that disappointed little pout. Besides, he was mad at Dean for being crass. He could have said a polite *no, thanks* without shoving it in Nikki's face that he'd never loved her. At least not as much as Mary Ann. He must not have wasted any time in saying *I do* once the two of them hooked up again.

She met his gaze. "You wouldn't believe what he said about you."

"*Me?*"

"Yeah, and that was before he knew you were in the park."

Jack leaned toward her. "What did he say?"

She blinked hard. "Just that it would be impossible for me to form a real relationship with *any* man as long as Jack was along."

"Hey!" He didn't know why, but he didn't like the sound of that. Then, secretly, he wondered if it was true. If the roles were reversed, he wasn't sure he'd be so understanding.

"Ludicrous, right? What an inane thing to say."

"Totally stupid."

"Then, when he saw you were here, he really flipped out."

"I caught that part."

She heaved a sigh and shivered.

"We need to get you out of the rain."

"Yeah, and you've got to go to work." The truth was, he did. He was already an hour late, but he knew the boss would cut him slack. His boss was not just his dad, he was also one of Nikki's biggest fans. Plus, he was a huge proponent of helping out distressing damsels. Yeah, he said it that way because he knew Nikki was the one who gave Jack the biggest headaches. He also thought she was funny and sweet and *"just as cute as a button."* He'd known her since she was a kid, when she and Jack had first started hanging out.

"When do you go in today?"

"Four o'clock."

"Night shift?"

"Yeah."

"Stop by later for some fish and chips? I'll even toss in a draft beer." Jack helped his dad run a restaurant by the water. His dad managed the place while Jack kept the books. One day, his dad hoped to turn the operation over to Jack completely, and Jack wouldn't be opposed. He loved chatting with the customers at The Wharf and had a great time shooting the breeze with the fishermen who brought in their daily catches.

"Girl can't refuse an offer like that." She flashed him a smile, and his whole world seemed warmer. "Besides, we've got to plan our next move."

"Move?"

"Jeremy," she answered, like that was so logical he should have thought of it.

"Oh right," he said, his heart sinking a bit. "Jeremy."

"Ow! Watch it, will ya?"

Nikki pulled back the straight pin, realizing she'd just poked the poor man's shoulder. She was taking the jacket in to adjust for the slope in his shoulders, as well as for the fact that one of his arms was longer than the other.

"I'm sorry, sir. I'll try to be more careful."

He studied her in the mirror with cool, gray eyes. "Yes, do that, won't you?"

Nikki's face heated under his stern gaze. She couldn't afford to mess this up. She'd already had two customers complain to her boss today.

She nodded and continued marking the seam, taking extra care with her work. She finally finished, then adjusted the jacket. "Better?"

He turned to study his own reflection, pivoting from side to side. "I think it's an improvement. Don't you?"

"You look exceptional," she said in her best, polished tone.

He eyed her skeptically.

"No, seriously. The cut is perfect on you now."

He shook out his arms, then turned to get a rear view, glancing over his shoulder. "You're right!" He surprised her with a smile. "It works."

Nikki smiled in return, sighing inwardly with relief.

"How soon can you have this ready?"

"Tuesday?"

He twisted his lips, then pulled a billfold from his pocket and extracted some cash. He pressed a large bill into her hand. "Can I convince you to have it ready by tomorrow?"

Nikki looked down in shock to see it was a hundred. "Sir, I can't—" She tried to hand it back to him, but he nodded her off.

"Nonsense. I know it's extra work: a rush job."

She attempted to return the money again. "I really can't accept tips."

"It's not a tip. It's an incentive."

She met his eyes. "Incentives either."

"That's too bad." He plucked the bill from her fingers. "Then I'll have to take my business elsewhere." He removed the jacket and handed it to her as she stood there dumbstruck.

"Wait!" she called as he turned to go. "I can have it ready tomorrow. No extra incentives necessary."

He studied her. "By noon?"

Nikki felt sweat bead at her temples. Noon would mean either staying late or coming in very early. She already had three other orders to finish and had fallen behind due to her time away. If she lost another customer today, her boss would have her head. Marilynn had been less than enthusiastic about her taking time off for her aunt's funeral. The day after Christmas was big for sales, and the other tailor they employed, Roger, was on a cruise in the Caribbean that he'd booked months in advance. Nikki had promised to hold down the fort during the holidays, but she couldn't have foreseen her family emergency. She equally couldn't have known she'd return from the Midwest such a mess.

It was hard to focus on her job with Mallory's deadline looming overhead. If she got that inheritance, she might not need this job at all. But at the moment, the prospect of two million dollars seemed like pie in the sky, and Nikki needed to keep her feet on the ground. Her mom's supervisors were even less understanding than Marilynn, and that spoke volumes. They'd said that if Emma had to keep taking days off due to her health, perhaps it would be best for her to think of not coming back at all. Times were tough, and plenty of others needed employment. Others who could be relied on to come in to work day after day.

No matter how independent her mom tried to be, Nikki knew that if push came to shove—and she really did lose her job—Emma couldn't support herself and Tony on unemployment, even with him keeping his part-time job. Nikki would have to step in and help out. And she'd be glad to. She'd take on added work if that was what her mom and Tony needed to make ends meet. But the best way to earn extra cash involved working overtime here. That would prove impossible if she lost this job. Nikki swallowed hard, then met the customer's gaze. "Tomorrow at noon will be fine."

Once he'd gone, Marilynn leaned her head into the fitting room. She wore a short, blonde bob and little tiny glasses that set severe dark lines against her steely gaze. "At least you didn't mess that last one up. He actually *complimented you* on the way out."

Nikki blinked and smiled politely, holding her tongue. While she'd gotten on famously with the old boss who had hired her, Marilynn had been on her case since day one. Nikki didn't even know why. She worked hard and was generally good at her job.

"Oh, and since you'll be coming in early tomorrow anyway…"

Nikki held her breath and waited, expecting the ambush. When Marilynn began a sentence with "Oh…" it typically meant one was coming. "You might want to take a second look at those gabardine slacks you hemmed."

"But they're all done. Set for pickup."

"Not quite." Marilyn wagged her index finger. "I took a look at the stitching, and frankly…" She shared a twisted smile. "I found it a bit uneven."

"But, I—"

"No *buts* about it," Marilyn scolded sternly, as if Nikki were some wayward preschool child. "You know how we feel about quality control at Stanley's." Her voice took on a sing-songy tone. "I wouldn't want to have to mention anything to the higher-ups about someone getting sloppy."

Nikki met Marilynn's gaze. "I'll look at the slacks," she told her. "First thing."

Later that evening, Nikki sat at the bar with Jack. He'd poured them both draft beers before putting in her order. The place was closing up, with just a few scattered diners lingering at their tables. Nikki could understand the patrons' reluctance to leave. The view of the harbor was stunning from here, particularly at night with lights dotting the docks and twinkling from nearby establishments. She took a swig from her mug, then set it down. "Marilynn was extra feisty today."

"Uh-oh, don't tell me she used the 'O' word."

"As in *Oh, Nikki…*?" Nikki took another sip of beer. "Yeah, she did."

"What've you done now?"

"Oh, Jack—"

"Now you're using the 'O' word on me."

She burst out laughing. "Not like she does, and you know it."

"Right." He quaffed his own drink. "So tell me. What's the infraction?"

"Gabardine slacks."

"Sounds serious."

"More serious than I knew."

He stroked his chin. "Too long in the crotch?"

She swatted him.

His brow shot up. "Too short?"

"Stop it!" But she was giggling just the same.

"You can't let her get to you. Just think of her as an unpleasant aspect of your job. Necessary but unpleasant."

"I wouldn't call her necessary."

"What would you call her, then?"

"Resident evil."

Jack chuckled behind his mug just as his dad, Greg, appeared. "Nikki!" he said, holding his arms out for a hug. "Aren't you a sight for sore eyes?" Greg looked just like Jack only about thirty years older, plus about twenty pounds heavier. His brow was wrinkled and his hair was thinning, but he was one of the kindest men Nikki knew. He embraced her sweetly, then pulled back with a frown, his face etched with concern. "I'm sorry for your loss, kiddo."

"Thanks, Greg."

"How was the trip? Jack here says it was a whirlwind."

"We were pretty much up and back."

"And the service?"

"A little lonely."

"Lonely, huh? I'm sorry to hear that."

"Her Aunt Mallory didn't have many friends," Jack said.

Greg gave Nikki's arm a pat. "Well, at least she left good family behind her. And family, as we all know, means everything."

Nikki smiled sadly. "Yeah."

Greg glanced at their beers. "All taken care of? Got something to eat?"

"It's coming, thanks," Nikki answered.

"Well, you let me know if there's anything I can do for you, kiddo. Anything at all." He glanced at his son. "Meanwhile, I'll leave things in Jack's capable hands." He met Nikki's eyes. "You know he has your back."

"I know that, and I'm very grateful."

Another middle-aged man approached Greg and held out his hand with a loud hello. Greg turned toward him, smiling brightly. "Well, I'll be a monkey's uncle!"

"See you later!" Nikki said as he left them.

Greg shot her a wink before walking away with his long-lost chum. "Hope so."

Just then, Nikki's cell rang. "It's my mom," she said, checking the number.

Jack nodded as she took the call.

"Hey, Ma. How are you feeling?"

"Good, Nikki. I'm good. I was just calling to see how things went at Aunt Mallory's."

"It…was a busy trip."

"Jack went with you?"

She eyed him sitting beside her at the bar. "Yes."

"That's good. I'm glad you had company for the road." There was a brief pause on the line before her mom continued. "I'd like to hear more about it. I was thinking that maybe you could come to dinner. You can bring Jack if you'd like."

Nikki covered her cell with her hand. "She wants you to come to dinner."

"Just me?"

Nikki glared at him because he never stopped teasing, but he knew her ire was pretend.

"Fine. Yes. I'll go… When?"

"When were you thinking, Ma?"

"Friday."

Nikki glanced at Jack. "It's New Year's Eve," she whispered. "Maybe you have plans?"

"No plans I can't cancel."

"Seriously?" she asked, her cell still covered.

"Nikki," he told her firmly. "I'm not sending you in there to spill to your mom alone."

"Who says I'm spilling to my mom?"

"You're not planning to tell her?"

"Not planning to tell me what?"

Nikki looked down to see her hand had slipped off the mouthpiece. "It's nothing," she answered quickly, "nothing at all." Then she said her good-byes and stared at Jack. "I don't want Emma knowing anything."

"About the will?"

She shook her head.

"But why not?"

"She'll say it's crazy, just one more way Aunt Mallory is trying to manipulate things from the grave."

"And she'd be right!"

Nikki's fish and chips arrived, and boy did they smell heavenly. "Jack, I don't want my mom knowing anything, including anything about what happened in the park today. Because she'd tell me to stop, try to talk me out of it."

"Selling yourself off for cold, hard cash?"

Nikki's temperature spiked. "Hey, listen. I do not sell out, okay?" she said, remembering her earlier client. "At least not in the way you're thinking. You believe this is all about me, don't you? That I'm somehow being selfish." Moisture built in her eyes, but she fought back her tears. "Sometimes Jack, there's a nobler cause, you know. Something that is bigger than ourselves."

He met her gaze. "It's not up to you to set the world right."

"Not your world, maybe. But in my little universe? Yeah. I'm taking control." She picked up a bottle of malt and sprinkled it liberally on her fried fish.

"Hey," Jack said softly. "I'm not the enemy."

She stopped what she was doing to look at him.

"I'm the one who's here for you, remember? The one who has your back?"

Nikki knew it was true. There was nobody else she could count on. No one else she'd trust with her deepest secrets, especially the ones she was harboring now.

"I won't say a word to your mom about the whole Mallory thing. I promise."

"I couldn't wish for a better friend."

Jack's eyes glistened slightly in the dim light. "Neither could I." He surprised Nikki by reaching into his jeans pocket and pulling out a small, wrapped package. He set it on the bar in front of her beside her steaming plate. "A few days late, but…Merry Christmas."

Nikki was overwhelmed by emotion, and embarrassed for having snapped at him. "You didn't."

"I have to get you back somehow." He shot her a tilted smile. "For those amazing concert tickets."

She lifted the tiny box in her hand. It was professionally wrapped like it had come from a jeweler's. "I hope you didn't break our pact."

"By getting you anything too expensive or personal?"

She stared into his deep brown eyes and slowly nodded.

"Nope."

"Well, good."

"Nothing's too expensive—or too personal—for a best friend."

"Jack!"

"Okay, okay. The truth is I might have stretched the limits just a bit. But it was for very good reasons."

"I'm listening."

"Remember last spring when we were talking about relationships? About what makes them perfect?"

"Romantic relationships, you mean?"

"Yeah. It was just after you broke up with Dean."

"He dumped me."

"His loss."

"Thanks."

"Both times."

"Can we cut to the chase here?" She rattled the present, ready to open it. There was nothing Nikki loved more than gifts, and she rarely received any. Usually she was the one making stuff for other people. Handmade stuff, but still. It really *was* the thought that counted.

"We both laid out our criteria. Yours were a little more picky than mine."

"Precise, Jack. I believe the word is *precise*. You said that setting expectations didn't really matter. When you found the one, you knew it somehow. It was like fate, karma…destiny. And I said there's more to it than that. The two people should be compatible in three important ways. A melding of mind, body, and—"

"Spirit," he finished for her.

She studied his face for clues but couldn't find any answers. "What's this about?"

"Open it."

She carefully slid off the silky ribbon, then peeled back the shiny red paper. It was a jewelry box. Nikki's heart pounded. He couldn't have… Shouldn't have… She lifted the lid to find a lovely necklace nestled inside. "Oh Jack, it's beautiful."

"It's an infinity charm," he told her.

Nikki held the charm up by its silver chain, seeing three thin metal bands braided around each other and coiled into a circle.

"That's white gold, yellow gold, and silver."

"Mind, body, and…" Nikki choked back a sob, overcome by the moment.

"I was thinking if you wore it, it might bring you luck. In finding the right guy."

"And right now, I need all the luck I can get."

"No, you don't." He looked at her with compassion. "All you've got to do is be yourself."

"Do you really think I can do it? Find that sort of person between now and February?"

"You may have to lower your standards a little."

"What?"

"I bought you the necklace before Christmas, Nikki. Before I realized you were on a deadline."

Her head wrestled with her heart, but her head ultimately won. "Two out of three's not bad."

Jack studied her pretty profile, wishing he could find a way to convince Nikki not to settle. But when Nikki was determined, there was no convincing her of anything.

"Which two are you going for?"

"The two I can get, I guess."

He watched her a moment, then said quietly, "Your food's getting cold."

"Oh yeah." She dropped the necklace back in the box and replaced its lid. "Thanks for the necklace, Jack. I really love it. I love it a lot."

She took a bite of her cod and it crunched, steam escaping. "So, what did you get Veronica?" she asked, referring to his girlfriend.

"A digital camera, like she wanted."

"That was nice."

"Yeah." *Especially now that she's out of the picture*, Jack thought but didn't say. They'd had a big fight the night he returned from Mallory's funeral. Veronica hadn't liked him going away, and he wouldn't give in to her demands for him to stop seeing his best friend. What's more, Jack understood he'd emerged from the trip conflicted. He couldn't keep seeing Veronica when he felt so mixed up about Nikki. As if her caving in to her aunt's demands for her to marry another guy wasn't bad enough, their exchange in that motel room had jumbled his emotions. He had to sort out his own head before getting involved with any female—ever again.

"How are you going to explain New Year's to her? Won't she be upset about it?"

"No more than she is already."

Her face registered understanding. "You didn't. Right before Christmas?"

"It was after, actually. She took it okay." He shrugged. "Maybe all she wanted was that camera anyway."

"Come on."

"I spoke with Dave," he said, changing the subject.

"Your cousin the lawyer?"

"Yeah."

"When?"

"Today, after the park."

"And?"

"He says maybe there's a way out of it. We... You can contest, just like your aunt's counsel said."

"How long will that take?"

"At least a couple of months. Maybe more."

"That's cutting things awfully close."

"Yeah, but it could work. You could still get the money and not have to go through with any of this."

"That sounds like a pretty big *if* from this stool."

"I think it's an angle worth pursuing."

"How much will it cost?"

"I can get him to cut you a deal."

"I doubt I can afford it."

"I'll talk to him."

"I don't know." But she looked like she was considering it. "What if I miss the boat, and the whole wad goes to the state?"

"It's a risk, I know. But—"

She looked him square in the eye. "I'm not willing to take a risk."

"Nikki, listen to me. One week ago, you didn't even know about the money. Now that you do, you're whole life's gone crazy."

"No. Now that I do, my life's got potential. Potential beyond what I ever dreamed possible. I can *do something* for my mom and brother, Jack. Finally give back."

"And sacrifice yourself in the process?"

"It won't be a sacrifice."

"How do you know?"

She laid her hand on the present he'd given her. "If I don't at least feel a full two out of three, I won't do it."

"You mean there has to be something there besides the money?"

"I mean I have to believe I can actually *love* the guy. I'm not a robot, you know. I have a heart beating in here." She thumped her chest with her fist. "All I'm saying is, there are people I've loved in the past. What's so wrong about believing I could maybe love them again? It happened to Dean with Mary Ann, didn't it?"

There was nothing Jack could say to that. In a very strange way, Nikki was almost starting to make sense.

"It could all work out. Can't you see? Maybe I and one of my exes didn't make it for a reason. That reason could be as simple as timing."

"And who knows?" Jack interceded. "Maybe you haven't even found him yet. Your soul mate. You still could run into him. There's time."

"You're right." Nikki reopened the gift box and took out the necklace. "Here," she said, handing it to him. "Help me put this on."

Nikki lifted her hair, and he draped the delicate chain around her neck, clicking its latch in place. The eternity charm dipped toward her cleavage as it hung in the opening of her V-neck sweater. She looked up at him with big, blue eyes and smiled. Jack had always found her pretty, but she seemed extra beautiful in this moment.

"I like it. I think it's going to bring me luck."

He smiled back at her, thinking this was going to be one hell of a ride. "What time should I come to get you on Friday?"

"I'll probably have to go straight there from work. Still got lots of catching up to do."

"Pick you up a six o'clock?"

"Better make it seven."

Chapter Four

Jack held open the door, and Nikki slid into the passenger side of his car. "Did you bring the list?"

He sighed heavily. "Yeah, I've got it." During the few days they'd been apart, Nikki had tasked Jack with making up a master list of all potential *candidates*. She was creating her own roster, and then they were going to compare.

She set her bag on the floor and buckled up before studying his list. "Herbie McLondon? You've got to be kidding!"

"You said to think back."

"Not back to the second grade. How did you remember him anyway?"

"Because you told me he was your only redhead. Typically, you're attracted to darker guys."

She tried not to look at him. "Dean was blond."

"Yeah, so? But how many others? Go on," he said smugly. "Check the list."

Nikki stared out the window, where light snow was drifting. "That's silly. I don't even believe in that whole *type* thing."

"Me either."

"Right," she said with a laugh. "Your type I could peg to a tee."

"Could you now?" He turned to look at her when he pulled up to a stoplight. "Let's hear it."

"Blonde, skinny, and stacked."

"That's patently unfair."

"The greatest predictor of future behavior is past, Jack."

What Nikki didn't know was that Jack *did* have a type. Any type that didn't remind him of her. It seemed better that way, keeping things completely separate. There were the girls he would date, the ones he would sleep with, and then there was—

"Gosh!" she shouted suddenly. "I'd forgotten all about Brett!"

"He was the banker, wasn't he?"

"Good call, Jack. He might have slipped my mind completely."

"Maybe that's because you only went on one date."

"Yeah, but it was a good one."

"Hmm."

"What's that supposed to mean?"

"You didn't go on a second."

"That's because he was allergic to cats."

"You don't *have* cats, Nikki."

"No, but I might get one someday. Or I might have a kid who wants one."

"You always were a long-term thinker."

"I know what you're saying. Maybe I should scratch him off the list?"

"Maybe."

"Herbie too?"

"Nikki, that was a joke!"

"Oh."

She took a pen from her purse and drew a line through both names. Oops! She must have spotted Dean's name there at the top. She lifted her pen and scratched his name out too. "You didn't have to include this first one."

"You said to be thorough. Besides, I thought it best to keep a complete record."

"Why?"

"Perhaps you'd like to share it with your kids someday. You know, those cat-loving kids? The names of all their might-have-been dads."

"Shut up and drive."

"Yes, ma'am." But he was chuckling. Damn, she was fun to be around. If only some other guy didn't have to be reminded of that fact.

Nikki glanced over her shoulder at a brown paper sack on the backseat. "What's in the bag?"

"I brought a bottle of champagne along. It's New Year's Eve."

"That's very sweet. I'm sure my mom will appreciate it."

"I was thinking we could pop it in the fridge when we get there."

"Better make it the freezer. It will chill faster."

A little while later, Emma opened the door to her brownstone. Nikki was struck at once by how thin she appeared. Since the last time she'd seen her, her mom must have dropped ten pounds, and that was only three weeks ago.

"Nikki!" Emma cried happily. "Jack!" She gave them both warm squeezes and welcomed them inside. "I'm so glad you could make it. It's the first chance I've had to see you over the holiday." She took Jack's coat as Nikki hung her own in the closet. "I hope you don't mind Christmas dinner. Tony and I were waiting on you."

"I thought I smelled turkey roasting."

"Corn pudding and stuffing too," Emma assured him.

"Smells delicious."

"Yeah, Ma. Thanks." She studied her mom's face with worry, knowing she must have worked extra hard to pull off a full-scale holiday meal. "But you shouldn't have gone to the trouble."

"I made the pies," Tony said, appearing in the foyer.

"Hey, buddy." Jack shook his hand. "Cooking now, are we? That's one way to impress the ladies."

"It's also a way he can learn to feed himself." Nikki hugged her little brother tightly. "Though, gosh, Tony, it feels like you're eating enough! Are you working out or something?"

He demurred but grinned proudly. "I've been pressing some, yeah."

"That's another way to impress the ladies," Jack said with a laugh.

"Will you stop it already," Nikki ribbed him. "He's only seventeen. He doesn't even have a girlfriend."

"Oh yes, he does," Emma said sweetly, disappearing into the kitchen. Seconds later, she emerged with a pretty teenage girl. "Nikki, Jack, I'd like you to meet Holly."

Nikki's jaw dropped. Jack reached over and shut it before speaking first. "Nice to meet you, Holly."

"Yeah, me too," Nikki said, still a little stunned.

"Let's all go into the kitchen and catch up while I put the finishing touches on dinner."

"We'll help set the table, Mrs. Constantino," Holly offered helpfully. She shot a pointed glance at Tony.

"Right," he said, picking up on her cue. "We will. Right now."

Nikki's mom's face blossomed in a happy smile. Despite her wan appearance, she seemed content to be around her family. "Thanks, kids."

"Looks like he got a winner," Nikki whispered to Jack as they entered the kitchen and the kids slipped away.

"Yeah," he answered. "But she's pretty lucky too."

Jack handed his champagne to Emma. "I brought us some bubbly for after dinner."

"How nice, Jack." She shot Nikki a look and clucked. "Looks like you nabbed a winner yourself." She took the bottle from Jack and popped it in the fridge, and Nikki flushed.

Her mom was always dropping hints about how she and Jack should be together. *As if...* Nikki wasn't even Jack's type! As long as Nikki had known him, Jack had jumped from one relationship to another like some kind of wild jackrabbit. Even if the girl seemed perfect, he always found some fault with her. And his faultfinding times generally coincided with the woman wanting to get too close. Go out for some laughs, have a great time... Sure. Ask Jack for his apartment key? Like that was going to happen. Nikki was surprised enough that she had it.

I think we'd better put it in the freezer," she said, taking the bottle out of the refrigerator and sliding it behind the door on top.

"Might explode," her mom cautioned.

"We'll watch it," Nikki assured her. She turned her attention toward the stove, where a deliciously browned turkey sat cooling. "Yum! Should I make the gravy?"

"That would be great."

"Can I carve the bird?" Jack smiled at Emma, and Nikki hated him for being so congenial. Every time he dropped by, her mom only liked him more. If she understood their relationship, that would be fine. But the fact was she didn't. *"In my day, men and women couldn't be friends,"* she was fond of saying. *"At least not without one of them secretly liking the other."*

Nikki stared at Jack, and he raised an eyebrow, like *what's up?* But she just shook her head as if her mom's suspicions were ridiculous. She and Jack, hoo! Jack and her? Ha-ha. He turned to pull a knife from the block by the stove, and muscles rippled beneath his button-down shirt. In a flash, Nikki was reminded of the feel of his body pressing hers. And the look in his eyes as his mouth hovered just above hers.

"Nikki," her mom said. "Didn't you hear me? I asked you to get Jack the platter."

"The platter, right." Nikki swallowed hard. "The big one with the turkey on it?"

"That's the one."

Jack glanced at her over his shoulder. "Is something wrong?"

Nikki brought her palms to her cheeks, realizing they had to be bright red. "No. Yes. I mean, I just had a flash of heat—"

"You're too young for that," Emma cut in.

"From the kitchen."

Jack eyes danced. "Well, you know what they say…"

"I'm leaving!" Nikki blurted out just a little too loudly. "On my way to the sideboard." But when she passed through the swinging door, she caught Tony and Holly kissing under the mistletoe. She coughed, and the kids broke apart. "Setting the table. Right."

Tony gestured to the elegant place settings the two of them had already laid out. "We're all done."

"Great." Nikki grinned and took out the turkey platter. "Then join us in the kitchen. I'm sure there's still lots to do."

As she got to know Holly over dinner, Nikki saw she was actually very nice, and appeared smart as well. Who would have thought it! Her baby brother, having a girlfriend already! Then again, when she looked at him, he suddenly seemed more like a man. He'd broadened across the shoulders and his face had matured quite a bit in these last few years. He could nearly pass for a college boy. Nikki's heart sank at the thought, knowing how badly he wanted to go. She didn't dare bring it up, because it was a sore spot. Most college admissions deadlines had already come and gone, and Tony had missed them all. He was determined to work a year or two after high school, save up money, and then apply. But Nikki knew the cold, hard reality. Most people who started that way never went to college at all. They got busy with day-to-day struggles in paying their bills. The last thing on their radar was taking out loans and becoming further indebted for undetermined results. But maybe she was projecting. Unfairly comparing her life to her little brother's.

Jack lifted the Chianti bottle on the table and offered to fill Emma's empty glass.

She declined with a shake of her head. "Thanks, I'd better not."

"No wine tonight?" Nikki asked her, noticing she hadn't had a drop. While her mom had never been a big drinker, she often had a glass with dinner.

"The medication," she whispered softly. "Can't mix it."

Nikki frowned as Emma motioned toward the mashed potatoes. "Mind passing those over?" she said to Tony, whose face also registered concern. Their mom had given herself a birdlike serving to begin with.

At least she was attempting to have some more. Tony met Nikki's eyes with a worried gaze and lifted the serving dish. But when Emma tried to take it, its weight sank heavily in her hands. "Oh!"

Jack reached out and grabbed the dish just before it crashed to the table. He glanced at Nikki before returning his attention to her mom. "You okay?"

She rubbed the back of her neck. "Just a little tired tonight."

No wonder, Nikki thought. She'd totally overdone it with the food. The portions were large too, which meant the baking pans and casserole dishes had been extra heavy to maneuver.

"Tony, Holly, do you think you could clear the table?"

"Sure," Tony said, standing.

"I thought you wanted more potatoes?" Nikki interrupted.

Emma appeared defeated. "I'm done."

All of a sudden, Nikki felt like she was going to burst out crying. This wasn't the mom she remembered. The one she recalled was a fighter. Someone who didn't give up.

Holly got to her feet as well. "Everything was awesome, Mrs. Constantino. Thanks so much."

Emma smiled weakly as the kids gathered the empty plates. When they'd gone, she spoke to Nikki. "I didn't want to ask in front of the kids, but how were things at the farm?"

Nikki's gaze flitted to Jack, who sat there with his lips pressed tightly together. "Um, it was fine. Everything went fine."

"And the service?"

"It was quiet."

This didn't seem to surprise Emma. "Did Mallory make arrangements for her estate?"

"Arrangements?" Nikki asked, purposely naïve.

"She had quite a spread. A dairy, wasn't it?"

"Yes," Jack added helpfully. "Lots of cows. Some very big ones."

Nikki stared at him.

"What's going to happen to the cows?"

Nikki returned her gaze to her mother. "I, uh… We're hoping…"

Jack could see Nikki was stuck. She'd never been much good at keeping things from her mom. "Seems like Mallory made some plans."

"What kind of plans?"

"Plans to have the cows looked after," Jack stated matter-of-factly.

"Oh," Emma answered, clearly not understanding. "Well, that's good."

"Yes," Nikki stepped in. "She made plans for settling her whole estate. Only, that's going to take a while."

Emma's eyebrows rose.

"Probate," Jack explained. "Apparently, these things can take months to work themselves out."

"That's too bad," Emma said. "For your sake," she told Nikki, "I was hoping there'd be at least a little bit of money."

"Ma!"

"You work so hard, honey. And for that horrible woman. What's her name?"

"Marilynn," Jack filled in.

"Yes, her. She's done nothing but ride you since she took over. I know you try to hide it, but I can see how miserable you've been."

A lump welled in Nikki's throat. "It's not so bad."

"Baloney! I wish you could leave that place."

"That makes two of us," Jack added.

Nikki felt on the verge of tears. Here her mom was worried about *her*, when Emma was the one who really needed the money. "I'm going to hit the restroom real quick," she said, rising from the table. She passed Tony and Holly in the kitchen. They had on their winter coats. "Leaving already?"

"There's a New Year's party at Rick's," Tony told her. Rick was Tony's best friend, and forever getting him into mischief. Nikki just hoped tonight wasn't one of those times. Then again, her little brother had matured quite a bit and seemed like he could take care of himself.

"Oh, okay. Have fun."

"Nice meeting you, Nikki," Holly said with a pleasant smile.

"Yeah, Holly. You too."

Then, while the kids went to say good-bye to the others, she hightailed it to the bathroom. Once there, Nikki caught her breath and leaned into the counter. Falling apart now wasn't going to help anybody, least of all her mom.

She slowly raised her eyes to the mirror and spied the arsenal of prescription bottles lined up before it. It had to cost a fortune to keep her mom in all those pills, and none of them appeared to be working. She didn't know how she was going to get through the rest of this night without breaking down. But she needed to be strong for her mom's sake. Nikki thanked the heavens she had Jack there beside her. At least she wasn't going through this by herself. Jack would never leave her to face something like this alone. While he'd resisted the idea of her going along with her aunt's demands in the beginning, he seemed to be coming around. He'd gone with her to the park, hadn't he? He'd even thought hard over compiling that list. After seeing her family tonight, Nikki was convinced more than ever that she was doing the right thing in trying to secure her inheritance. That money could help so many people in so many ways. Plus, it would help Big Mama.

When Nikki returned to the dining room, she was stunned to see Jack standing and holding both their coats. "What's going on?"

"Your mom needs to rest," Jack said with a worried frown. "I told her we'd push off and let her have some quiet."

"But the dishes?" Nikki protested.

"Those can wait," Emma answered. She seemed to be holding things together as best she could, but Nikki could see her mom was ready to break down herself. She obviously didn't want Nikki and Jack to see it, which was why she was urging them to go.

"Well, if you're sure?" Nikki asked uncertainly.

Emma nodded, and Jack held up her coat so she could slip it on.

"Don't forget about that bottle," Jack warned Emma.

"Oh no!" her mom cried. "The champagne!"

Nikki dashed to the kitchen and pulled the icy bottle from the freezer. The cork had tried to push itself out but was prevented from popping by the twisted metal wires that held it in place.

"Better take that with you," Emma said. She looked at Jack. "It was a very sweet gesture. Thank you, but I won't be having any myself."

Jack held the champagne bottle under his coat as he and Nikki walked through the snow toward the park. It was coming down harder now, pelting their hats and shoulders with heavy wet flakes. Nikki's cheeks were flushed, her nose crimson. Still, when he'd asked where she wanted to go, she said she needed some air. "You sure you want to do this?" he asked. "I've got a gas fireplace back at my place."

"If it was a real one, you might talk me into it."

"What do you mean by real?"

"The old-fashioned kind, wood burning."

"Those suck the heat out of the building and pollute the air."

"Yeah, but they're much more romantic."

"You're in the mood for romance?" he asked playfully.

"Ha-ha."

His fingers were starting to feel numb clutching the chilly bottle, even through his warm leather gloves.

"Let's head over there." She pointed to an isolated bench at the hill's crest. It afforded a view of the outdoor skating rink ringed by lights. Couples glided across the ice hand in hand while groups of children clomped awkwardly past them. From this vantage point, they looked like miniature people in a snow globe, with white streaks raining down all around them.

Nikki trudged up the hill through the snow, and he followed after her. She dusted off the bench and motioned for him to sit. "So what do you think?" she asked, admiring the wintery landscape. Tree boughs hung heavy with snowdrifts, surrounding them in an enchanted forest.

His bottom met the frigid bench. "I think you're nuts."

"We'll warm up after a bit. Come on." She urged him closer. "Scoot over. And hand me some champagne."

Jack laughed and slid toward her. He pulled the bottle from beneath his coat and unwrapped its wires. Fitting his thumbs under the already swollen cork, he pressed it skyward. It flew from the neck of the bottle with a *whoosh*, sending foamy liquid bubbling down the sides of the bottle. Nikki giggled aloud as he held it away from him to keep his jeans from getting drenched. "Nice work!" she proclaimed, following the cork's trajectory into the darkness.

He handed her the bottle. "You do the honors."

She smiled and took a swig. "Brrr!" she said with a shiver. "Still cold!"

"It's meant to be served cold." She passed him back the bottle, and he took a long drink.

"Hey!" She swatted his arm. "Save some for me."

"There's plenty for you, Ms. Lightweight." In her younger days, that had gotten her in trouble, but she was older now and appeared to have grown out of it.

"You will never let me live down that night at the prom."

"It's hard to forget being attacked by a wildcat."

"I did… Hey! Watch it!"

"Well, you were," he said smugly. "Practically tore my tuxedo off. Ahhh, the memories."

"Billy Martin spiked the punch."

"I didn't recall him being in my car."

"Jack! We went together as friends, remember?"

"I'm not the one who seemed to forget."

He couldn't tell, but he thought she blushed in the darkness. She grabbed the bottle back from him and took another swig. "We sorted that out years ago. I was a little inebriated—"

"More than a little."

"Okay, fine. Pretty darn drunk. I didn't even know who you were, for crying out loud."

It was true, and Jack's heart ached at the memory. She'd even called him Chris, which was the name of the boy she'd had a crush on at the time. Jack suddenly regretted bringing this up. He'd burned for Nikki so badly that when she practically attacked him in the car, he thanked the heavens above for that opportunity. For the first time in two years, Nikki had finally come to her senses and could see Jack for who he was: an eligible high school senior who'd been hook-line-and-sinker crazy for her since the moment she first batted those eyes.

"Give me that champagne." Jack was embarrassed to hear his tone come out grumpy.

"What are you getting all cranky about? You're the one who wanted to take a walk down Memory Lane."

They each had a few more sips, then sat there in silence, staring through the slanting snow at the skaters down below.

"Nikki," he said at last, "I'm really sorry about Emma."

There was worry in her voice as she replied. "She looks bad, doesn't she?"

"Things seem to have gotten worse since I last saw her."

"I know." Nikki hung her head. "Me too."

Jack took the champagne bottle from her grip and wedged it into a pile of snow beside him. "I'm sorry. I know it must be hard. I don't know what I'd do if I saw my dad like that. He's always been so strong."

When she turned to him, there were tears in her eyes. "Ma's always been a tough one too. Only…" Her words fell off into soft sobs.

Jack raised her chin in his hand. "Nikki?"

"It seems like she's given up."

"Shhh, now. Hey, hey…" He pulled her to him in the drowning snow. "She's going to be okay. What she's got is fixable, yeah? It's not like some other things that—"

Nikki pushed back in his embrace to stare in his eyes. "That's why we have to fix it, Jack. *I* have to fix it, because I have a chance to."

Jack held her gaze, his heart breaking for her. He would do anything not to see Nikki in pain. Anything it took.

"Don't you see now? Understand a little better why my going through with Aunt Mallory's wishes doesn't seem so lame?"

He cupped her face in his hands and stroked back her tears. "I understand that you want to help." In a faraway universe, the music had stopped and a voice was issuing a countdown over the speakers by the ice rink. Ten… Nine… Eight…

Her mouth was inches away, its heat flowing toward him in the shadows.

"Then *help me* help, Jack. Please."

He drew closer, losing all sense of reason. Maybe it was the night or the champagne or the moment.

"What time is it?" she whispered.

"Almost midnight."

"Happy New Year!" rang out from the speakers below as hoots and hoorays echoed up the hill.

Jack was trapped in Nikki's gaze, unable to fight the tug of it. It was as if some invisible magnet was pulling him forward. Her lips trembled, and before Jack could think out what was happening, he claimed her mouth with his. He fell into her kiss, that warm and welcoming place he'd always imagined it to be.

"Jack!" Nikki said. "Don't!" But there was desire in her eyes. He couldn't mistake it. "I can't…" She pulled away from him. "We can't do this."

"Why not?" he asked, his voice husky.

"Because I need you."

"You have me. More than you know." He paused a beat. "Nikki, there's something I've been wanting to tell you—"

"No." She brought her hands to his lips. "Please. Don't." She blinked turning away. "It will only make it harder."

He didn't know how much harder things could get. They'd been damn near impossible forever.

There was pain in her eyes when she looked back at him. "Please don't make me tell you again, Jack. I love you. I've always loved you. But not like—"

"That," he finished for her.

He pulled the bottle from the snow and stood.

"Where are you going?"

"Home to get some shut-eye. It's as cold as Siberia out here. And I do mean polar."

Her face grew long. "You can't be mad at me for this. For something that you've known forever. Honestly, I thought you were over it."

"I am," he told her firmly. "I only kissed you just then because I thought you wanted me to."

"You what?"

"Come on, Nikki. You were giving me the signs."

"No. You imagined it."

"Doesn't really matter now, does it?"

"Why not?"

"Because," he said without skipping a beat, "you and I have work to do."

"You mean you'll...?"

"Yes. I'm going to help you finish this little task of yours to the bitter end." And he would too. In the past ninety seconds, he'd realized something absolutely, and the clarity stunned him. The only way he was ever going to move forward was by seeing Nikki firmly latched on to someone else. Her having boyfriends hadn't done it. It would have to be more serious than that. It would have to mean marriage. And for Nikki's sake as well as that of the guy involved—not to mention Jack's poor, battered heart—it was going to be a relationship that lasted. He was going to make sure of it.

She stared up at him, slack-jawed on the snowy bench.

"Let's get going," he told her. "Before we freeze to death out here."

"Thanks, Jack. For understanding."

"All I need to understand is that there were seven names on that list, and you've only crossed out three of them."

He picked up his pace, and she scurried down the path after him. "I don't even know where the others are!"

"Run an online search," he snapped over his shoulder.

"Okay." She stopped walking, and he turned to look at her.

"Aren't you coming?"

"You do want to do this? Because if not, I'm perfectly capable of—"

"Nikki, trust me on this. It will give me great pleasure to deliver you into another man's arms."

She swallowed hard. "If you're sure?"

"One hundred percent positive."

"And you're not mad?" she asked tentatively.

"Why would I be mad?" He blew an exasperated breath. "Look, it's already January first. Can't you see? While we're standing here blowing hot air, we're wasting time."

"You're right." She caught up to him, and they started walking again. "What's our next move?"

They approached his car, which was already piled over with snow, and he unlocked it. "You do a little bit of homework, and we'll meet up on Thursday for lunch. I can take some time off in the afternoon."

"And then?"

"Nikki, sweetheart." He grinned tightly and opened her door. "I don't have a crystal ball." But oh, how he wished he did. That way, he'd have a clue how soon this whole painful ordeal would be done.

"No, I suppose you don't. I don't guess either of us has."

Once she was settled inside, Jack shut her door and wiped the snow from the windshield with a scraper. Little by little he got the icy film shaved back until he could make out Nikki's hazy form through the glass. She sat there in the passenger seat, arms crossed to ward off the cold, looking as pretty as ever in that handmade hat. And in that instant, it hit him. *This is amazing! Unexpected! Awesome!* He was no longer in love with the girl. As beautiful as she was, she'd lost her particular appeal. A surprising weight lifted in his heart. After twelve incredibly long years, Jack Hudson was *free*.

Chapter Five

Nikki sat at her mom's kitchen table drinking coffee. It was Wednesday, her only day off, and Tony was in school. "What's up, hon?" her mom asked her. "You seem a little down today." Emma's face was drawn and pale.

"How are you feeling?" Nikki asked.

"I was asking about you."

"Yeah, but you're the one who called in sick."

Emma shifted, trying to conceal a groan. "Just woke up a little stiff, that's all."

"A little, Ma?"

Her mom's eyes brimmed with moisture. "Oh, Nikki," she admitted. "I don't know how much longer I can keep this up. I'm already having tingling in my leg."

"You what?" Nikki sprang from her chair. "We're getting you to a doctor. Now." She tried to grab for her mom's elbow, but Emma withdrew it.

"Settle down, honey and sit back down."

"But you said—"

"I know what I said, and I shouldn't have. Shouldn't have burdened you with the information. I'll be all right." She stared at Nikki and waited until she reluctantly took her seat. "The tingling passes after a while. As long as I stay still and stay off my feet."

Nikki wrung her hands. "You can't go on like this."

"The doctor's trying me on new medication. Maybe it will work."

"And if it doesn't?"

"He's got me lined up to start pain therapy."

"What does that mean?"

"They'll give me injections of cortisone. Right"— she pointed to the back of her neck—"here."

"Will that help?"

"Some patients get better completely."

Nikki studied her mom with a frown. This didn't seem probable in Emma's case. Not considering how long her condition had gone on and how it had worsened. Surgery was likely the only permanent remedy.

"You should sue Mel for doing this to you," she said, referring to her mom's boss at the diner.

"He didn't *make* me lift those heavy boxes, Nikki."

"Yeah, but when someone says 'it would be good if you could...' *and* that someone's your boss..."

Emma shook her head. "No way to prove it. This might even have been a preexisting condition, my doctor said. Something that was on the verge of happening anyway."

Nikki sighed heavily. "I still blame Mel, and now he's threatening to fire you on top of it."

Emma looked at her in sad agreement. "He's got a business to run."

"Maybe I should talk to him."

"Nikki, please. What good will that do?" She forced a weak smile. "Enough about me, all right? I want to hear about you."

Nikki toyed with her coffee cup, not looking up.

"Nikki?"

She raised her eyes to her mom's, not sure if she should broach the subject. Especially now when Emma wasn't feeling well. Maybe it was better to wait.

"Sweetheart, is something going on?"

"I don't know," Nikki answered honestly. She'd been so confused about things since New Year's Eve, she was still having trouble sorting them out.

"Is this about Jack?"

Nikki blinked. "How did you know?"

"Motherly intuition." Her mom reached out and gently stroked her arm. "What's going on, honey? Has something happened?"

Nikki blurted it out before she could stop herself. "He kissed me!"

"He what?" Emma brought a hand to her mouth to disguise a smile. "Well, my, my, my… It's about time, isn't it?"

"Ma!"

"What? Don't look at me like that. You can't pretend you haven't known, Nikki. That you couldn't see how he felt about you?"

Is he wearing a neon sign or something? "I… No! Absolutely not. We settled all that—back in high school."

"Doesn't sound like it was settled to me."

"Well, it was, okay?" Nikki said a bit too defensively.

"And?"

"And what?"

There was a mischievous twinkle in her mom's eye. "What was it like? The kiss?"

"I barely felt it," Nikki lied. "It happened so fast, you couldn't really call it a kiss. It was more like a peck. Yeah, like that."

"But on the lips." Why did her mom appear so amused? This wasn't funny.

"Yes, yes. Right here on my pecker." She pointed to her mouth. "There. Are you satisfied?"

"That's not for me to answer. I wasn't on the receiving end."

"Argh! It was nothing! Absolutely nothing. Okay?" She started to stand, but her mom stopped her.

"Then what are you getting so excited about?"

Nikki blew out a breath. "It was just…weird, you know? It was Jack. *Jack,* of all people!"

"I know."

"My best friend on earth!"

"I'm well informed about who Jack is. He may be your best friend, but that doesn't change facts."

"What facts?"

"That he's an eligible young man. Smart, funny, caring, and, oh yes…unbearably handsome."

"Ma!"

"Nikki, I may be fifty, but I still have eyes. I know attractive when I see it. And apparently so does every other female on the planet except for you."

"What on earth are you talking about?"

"You can't tell me you haven't noticed the way other girls are constantly playing up to him. I've seen them! A florist slipping him her number in a bouquet, when that bouquet was meant for someone else. The checkout girl at the market, asking leading questions about whether he's interested in cooking for two? The young woman at the bakery offering sugar with—"

"Okay. All right. I get it." But the truth was she didn't. Nikki only vaguely remembered those things. Perhaps that was because she hadn't been paying attention. Clearly not as much as her mom had. "Just where are you going with this?"

"I'm just saying that if Jack likes you—as more than friends—I think that's sweet. I also don't think you ought to take his affections for granted, Nikki. He won't be on the market forever, you know."

"Of course. I know of that. Neither of us is getting any younger. In fact, one of us is likely to marry soon."

Emma's eyebrows shot up. "One of you?"

"Statistically."

"It could also happen at once. I mean, for the two of you, if—"

"I don't feel that way about him. I never have."

Her mother eyed her carefully. "Haven't you?"

"No."

"You mean there was never a time, even one moment, where you thought that maybe you and he…?"

"No!" Nikki felt the fire of deceit in her cheeks. "It's not possible for a guy to be both to me. Jack's been my best friend for so long, I could never imagine him as something else!"

"As a lover, you mean?"

Nikki stared at her like *bite your tongue.* "He knows things about me," she cried with a gasp. "Knows that I rub cellulite cream on my thighs and wax my eyebrows!"

"That hasn't seemed to dampened his interest."

"Yeah, well," Nikki said sternly. "It sure has mine. Where would the romance be in that? A relationship based on the pure, unvarnished truth? Ew, gross, Ma. Come on! He's seen me in a mud mask, and on PMS. Seriously bloated—way out to here." She made a bulging motion in front of her stomach to demonstrate.

"I see what you mean. I suppose you've been privy to unsavory bits about him too."

Nikki stared at her mom and blinked. The truth was she couldn't think of anything really disgusting that Jack did. He wasn't as bad as most guys. Didn't strew his clothes around or dump wet towels on the floor. "He leaves the toilet seat up!"

"Heavens!"

"And… He sweats a lot."

"Sweats?" her mom asked with surprise.

"Yeah, when he works out."

"Nikki."

"He's a mess. Really. Totally gross."

Emma eyed her skeptically. "I'll bet all the girls at the gym think so too."

Nikki took a sip of her coffee and realized it had gone cold. "I don't like to think about Jack that way. I probably shouldn't have brought it up."

"Well, how did you leave things?"

"With Jack?" Nikki asked. "Oh, we left them just fine. We're going out to lunch tomorrow."

"As friends."

"Of course!"

"O-kay…"

"Ma, you're not to breathe a word of this. To anyone. All right?"

"Breathe a word of what?"

Nikki looked up as Tony entered the room, a backpack slung over his shoulder.

"Hey, hon," her mom said, "how was school?"

But Tony's gaze was on his big sister. "Does this have something to do with Jack?"

What? Did someone post a news bulletin around here? "Jack?" Nikki laughed lightly. "Don't be silly!"

"Oh, okay," he said with a shrug. "I just thought maybe you were discussing that mega-crush he's had on you since you were my age."

Nikki folded her face in her hands and lowered her head to the table.

"Sweetheart?" her mom asked. "Are you all right?"

She returned a muffled reply without lifting her head. "Fine, Ma. Just fine. Thanks for the motherly advice."

She heard a chair scrape the floor, then felt her mom's hand pat her back. "You're welcome, dear."

Nikki was inexplicably nervous about meeting Jack at the Burger Barn. She didn't know why. They'd eaten here lots of times before, and the food was always tasty. They even had a veggie burger on the menu, which was why she let Jack talk her into coming to this place. It was one of his favorites.

"Can I get you something to drink, miss?" the waitress asked. She wore a red-and-white-checkered apron with the face of a cheery cartoon cow on it. Seriously. What kind of cow would be happy about getting served up with fries? Certainly not Big Mama. Nikki heard a faint thumping against the table and looked down to see she'd been drumming it with her fingers. She slid her hand in her lap. "Just water for now. I'm waiting on someone."

As the waitress left, Nikki noticed a totally hot guy come in the door. He had a hunky build and rugged face with one of those crazy three-day beards like Hollywood actors wear. His head was covered in a knit cap dusted with snow. It hadn't stopped pounding since New Year's Eve. Good thing the city knew how to handle it. The waitress passed by him, telling him to sit anywhere. But as she scooted by, she stole a glance at the guy's behind. Really! Ogling—the guy pulled off his hat—*Jack?* He caught her eye and grinned, and something stirred inside her. Maybe it was nausea or indigestion. Or heartburn. Yeah, that. She should have nixed that third cup of caffeine.

Jack strode toward her with the self-assurance of a tiger. A tiger in a jungle he commanded as his own. Female heads swiveled in his direction, sharing appreciative glances. One woman scrawled a number on a paper napkin and held it toward him as he passed by. He snagged it without looking at her and tucked it in his pocket. No way! Her mom was right! He walked right up to Nikki and pinned her hand to the table with his leather glove. It was still damp from the snow outside.

"Been waiting long?" he asked, leaning toward her. His voice was a whiskey whisper, his dark eyes centered on hers.

"Just five minutes," she said with a squeak.

Nikki swallowed hard and stared down at their hands. She'd been doing it again. Tapping the table. Jack released his grip, and she wiped her damp hand with a napkin. He unzipped his parka and sat. "Parking was murder out there."

"New coat?"

Jack gripped the inside edges of his parka and fluffed it out. "What do you think? Is green my color?"

"Just like a jungle fern," Nikki muttered softly.

"What?"

Nikki blinked hard and pulled herself together. "I said, that's nice. What's it called? Desert Fern?"

Jack narrowed his eyes at her. "They have ferns in the desert?"

"Why sure," she said breezily. "Why not?"

The waitress appeared with Nikki's water and took their orders. "So," Jack said when she left. "Did you do your homework?"

"Are you growing a beard, Jack?"

He chuckled and stroked his chin. "Naw, just getting lazy. But, I don't know. Hmm. What do you think?" He cocked his chin from one side to another. "Should I keep it?"

"I think it looks…nice."

"Okay." He smiled and tucked his napkin in his lap. "I'll shave when I get home."

"Are you okay?"

"Great! How about you?"

"Good. I'm good, thanks," Nikki said unsurely.

"So, how about that research," he asked. "Did you do it?"

"I, uh…" Nikki felt totally lost, as if someone had changed the room on her but had forgotten to tell her about it. But that was nuts. They were still in the Burger Barn. Weren't they?

"Are you feeling sick or something?"

"I'm fine. Just fine." Nikki took a long swallow of water. "I was just thinking."

"Well, don't let it take too long. I've only got half an hour."

"What?"

He leaned toward her and whispered, "Meeting Angie for coffee."

"Who's Angie?"

"She's a florist down on—"

"Right. I remember." Nikki felt lightheaded. Probably from low blood sugar. She hoped their food would arrive soon and took comfort in the prospect that it would. Service was super fast here. She reached in her purse and pulled out the list.

"So what did you learn?"

"Jeremy and Kurt are still in the area."

"That's good."

"But Peter's in Rhode Island."

Jack massaged his chin, apparently liking the feel of all that stubble. "We can probably swing that for a day trip. Who else?"

"I couldn't find Brett through online searches at all."

"Not even in the White Pages?"

She shook her head.

"That's weird."

"Yeah."

"Anyway!" He smiled breezily. "We've got three to start with! How about Gordon?"

"I checked with Lanie, and Gordon's married." Lanie was an old work friend of Nikki's who had introduced her to her very attractive brother. He was in med school at the time but had since finished and married a fellow intern.

"See what happens when you let grass grow under your feet?"

"Grass?"

"You snooze, you lose."

Their food arrived piping hot, and Jack sank his teeth into his burger. "Hmm. Extra jalapenos, just how I like it."

Nikki, on the other hand, suddenly lost her appetite.

"What?" he asked her. "Not hungry?"

"Starved," she lied, picking up her veggie burger. She took a bite, but it was tasteless, something like cardboard served on whole wheat. That was odd. She'd always liked the food here before.

Jack polished off his burger while she watched him, forcing herself to nibble on hers.

"So?" he asked between chomps, "who's that leave?"

Her face fell in a frown. "Herbie McLondon."

"We'll save him as a backup."

His cell buzzed, and he checked it with a grin. "I hope you don't mind," he said, standing already. She suddenly realized he was leaving. Leaving her to go be with the flower girl. She'd probably decorated her bed in rose petals and lay there waiting for him in a negligee.

"No, go! Go on. Have fun!"

He pointed his finger at her as he backed toward the door. "Let's meet up on Saturday, your place, nine o'clock!"

Nikki nodded numbly.

"We'll tackle Jeremy then!"

"Jeremy, right!" she called, feeling her face flush.

Then he pulled his hat back on and whooshed out the door.

Jack stepped onto the street, noting a light spring in his step. A cold blast of air hit him square in the face, yet it was refreshing. Yes, indeed. Everything was looking brighter now that Nikki was out of his system. He didn't know why he'd wasted so much time pining for her. Sure, she was great, and dynamite to be around. But that didn't mean she was marriage material. It was as if a whole new world had opened up for him. For the longest time, he'd viewed the female populace as one great candy store: so many flavors to sample. The trouble with candy was you could only take so much of it before you had to rein yourself in. Things were different now. Jack had set aside his sweet tooth for more substantive pursuits. The ladies were now like a big, steaming buffet. Poached salmon… Rare roast beef… Garlic mashed potatoes. Things you could take your time with and linger over. Just the thought of it made him hungry, but Jack wasn't in the mood for food. He had a date with Angie, someone cute and funny and who obviously adored him. And, boy, didn't that feel good.

Chapter Six

Nikki stood outside Jeremy's apartment, the golden knocker looming ahead. Its swinging part was shaped like a musical note you lifted to bang against a treble clef plate. "Are you sure we shouldn't have called first?" she asked Jack, who stood behind her.

"Element of surprise. This is perfect."

"I don't know, Jack. Things didn't work out so well with Dean."

"That's because he knew you were coming."

"I thought it was because he was married."

"You're stalling."

She spun on her heels and stared up at him. "This isn't right. What am I supposed to say?"

"He's a rocker, right?"

"No. Peter's the rocker. Jeremy conducts the symphony."

"Same diff. Tell him you made beautiful music together."

Jack's cell buzzed in his pocket for the fifth time in the last ten minutes. Someone was texting him nonstop. "Can you turn that thing off?"

He checked the number, then silenced his phone. "Girl's crazy about me."

"You didn't shave," she said, noticing it for the first time.

"Angie thinks it's sexy."

"How do you do that? Get it to look the same?"

"Three-day setting on my shaver."

"There's a three-day…?"

He laid his hands on her shoulders and spun her back around. She was feeling overheated in her puffy white coat. The super of this building kept the halls unusually warm. Hers was such a cheapskate; she had to wear her coat around in her apartment—when the heat was turned on.

Nikki blew a hard breath that sent a loose lock of hair flying. Jack reached past her and pulled back the knocker, then let it slam. "Jack!" she hissed as he scurried toward the elevator. "Where are you going?"

He clasped his hands behind his back and started whistling. His eyes were fixed on the lighted numbers above. "Just waiting on the lift."

"You don't say *lift*," she whispered. "You're not Brit—"

Jeremy opened the door with a smile. "Brit? No. Quite American, darling. Nikki!" he said, extending his arms. "What a delight!"

Nikki glanced at Jack, who still pretended to wait on the elevator.

Jeremy gave her a perfunctory hug. "Well, for heaven's sakes. Come inside!"

Then he tugged her in the door and shut it at her back.

"I probably should have called."

"Nonsense! It's always a pleasure to hear from old friends." He strolled to the bar and lifted a bottle from a bucket. "Sherry? It's ice cold."

"Sure, thanks." She unzipped her coat and removed it, thinking he looked a little different somehow. His hair was really done. As in *done* done. Like he'd blown it dry, then styled it with a curling iron to set those wisps in place. "Did you change your hair?"

"Yes." He fingered the waves. "Do you like it?"

In truth, it looked a little weird. Like he'd worked way too hard. "Love it," she lied, still holding her coat.

"Just lay it over there," he said, indicating an armchair.

Nikki noticed the table in the next room was set for two with candles burning and everything.

"Oh gosh, you're expecting company."

"Yvonne won't mind."

"Yvonne?"

His cheeks took on a rosy glow as he motioned for her to sit. She sat on the cushy beige sofa, noting he'd had it recovered. She stroked the nubby fabric, savoring its texture. "Nice."

"You and I always had that in common," he said with a smile. "An appreciation for the finer things."

Nikki took a sip of her sherry and found it dry and crisp. It was likely expensive too.

"What brings you to the neighborhood?" he asked her.

"Why don't you tell me about Yvonne?" Nikki redirected.

"Oh well. *She* is fabulous."

"Yeah?"

"Super lovely. You'll see when she gets here."

"Oh no, I couldn't… Can't stay." Somehow, this was all wrong. Jeremy wasn't how she'd remembered him at all! Plus, he obviously had a new girlfriend. "I was just passing through this part of town, and I said to myself, I did. I said, Nikki, remember that fun guy you used to date?"

Jeremy preened like a peacock, toasting her with his glass.

"Maybe you should drop in and see him? See how he's been getting along."

"Isn't that the sweetest? Why, thanks, love." He laid his free hand on his chest. "From the bottom of my heart."

"How did you meet Yvonne?"

"She's in the orchestra. First violin."

"How great!"

"Nice hat," he commented. "Did you knit that?"

Nikki realized she'd failed to remove it and quickly took it off. "I, uh... Yeah." She fingered the scarf around her neck. "Matches this and my mittens."

"Mittens?"

"They're in the pockets of my coat."

"Well, it's a pleasure seeing you again. *Such* an unexpected pleasure." He took another sip of sherry and eyed her in an odd way. A little tingle raced down Nikki's spine. And not the good kind. "I have a feeling Yvonne will take pleasure in you too."

"Excuse me?"

"She's opened up a whole new world to me."

"Yeah?"

He lowered his voice and wiggled his eyebrows. "Delightfully wicked. Threesies and such."

Nikki sprang from her seat.

"Darling?"

"I just remembered I have an appointment!"

"Appointment?"

"With the podiatrist."

"What... Why?"

"Bunions," Nikki said, hobbling a little for effect. "Really, really bad ones."

"Oh no!"

"Yes. I can scarcely stand from the pain."

"You can't stand the pain?"

"That too!" she said, scooping up her coat.

"But this is so sudden," he said as she hurried for the door. "You've only just arrived!"

"I know! And it's been great!" She downed her last bit of sherry and set the glass on the table by the door. "Thanks for the drink!"

And then she slipped out the door and closed it as Jack turned to her in surprise. "What happened?"

"Let's go!" She stared at the elevator button. "It *still* hasn't come?"

A door creaked open, and Jeremy's voice called, "Oh, Nikki…?"

"Quick!" she said quietly. "The stairs!" Then she bolted for the exit with Jack trailing after her. How could she ever have loved that guy? Maybe she'd been flattered that he was older. Had found him worldly at the time. Jeremy got around much more than she knew!

"Slow down, will ya?" Jack said, nearly tumbling down the stairs. "Was he really that bad?"

"I'll tell you when we reach the car."

Jack was laughing so hard he couldn't get the key in the ignition.

"Will you stop it," Nikki said. "It's not that funny."

"No," he said with a chuckle. "It's hot. Way hot. Whoohoo, baby! Sizzle. Who knew that old croaker had it in him?"

"He is *not* that old, Jack."

"Oh yes he is. Pushing forty."

"Well, okay. So he's mature."

"Is that what you liked about him? I always wondered."

"I don't know what I liked, okay? The important thing is, it's over. There's no turning back with Jeremy."

"And Yvonne."

"Stop it."

"Maybe she's pretty. How do you know you wouldn't have…?"

Nikki soundly slapped his arm.

"Ow!"

"Shut up, you didn't feel that." His parka was at least an inch thick.

He finally inserted his key and cranked the engine. "Well, that didn't take long."

"It took long enough."

"Did he give you something to drink?"

"Why?"

"I thought smelled sherry."

"You're so suspicious."

"It's ten in the morning, Nikki."

"Okay, fine! I had one. I would have had two if I'd known what he was setting me up for."

"No wonder he was *delighted* to see you."

"Just drop me at work."

"Okay," he said, reaching in the glove box. He handed her a tiny white tin. "But first, you'd better have a breath mint."

Nikki entered the darkened department store, feeling disconcerted. Only the dim lights were on, with makeup girls busily checking the stock behind their counters. She breezed through the fragrance area, holding her breath. Thank goodness the men's department was in the back of the store. Her allergies couldn't take this constant assault. Even without customers present to spray sample bottles, the air was clogged with cloying scent. Nikki coughed and beelined for the back. She didn't know which was worse, gagging on old perfume or facing Marilynn.

"Good morning," Marilynn said, passing her with a clipboard. She'd probably been doing another one of her *inspections*. Marilynn delighted in invading employees' work areas when they weren't there, to write up their perceived infractions. She once scolded Nikki for creating a safety hazard by leaving a fully loaded pincushion on her sewing table. Seriously? It wasn't like she was watching toddlers back there. Who was going to get into them? Roger? He already had enough body piercings, thank you very much. Marilynn insisted he remove the rings while working, but she didn't know about *all* of them. Roger took silent pleasure in his secret rebellion.

"Morning," Nikki said crisply, passing by her.

Marilynn lowered her glasses as well as her tone. "I noticed you left out some pinking shears."

"Did I?"

"I'll have to write you up, you know."

Of course, she would.

"We can't have things getting sloppy."

"I'll try to be more careful."

"Let's hope so." There was an edge to her voice. "We're in the post-holiday slump now. Word is, some layoffs are coming."

Nikki turned to her with a gasp. "That's horrible."

"Odds are we'll only be able to keep one tailor on. So it will be either you or—"

Nikki's heart sank. "Roger."

"Yes."

Nikki couldn't believe how mean-spirited Marilynn was. She almost seemed to take pleasure in other people's misery. Roger was a single dad who really needed the job. Marilynn had never much liked him because he was a little alternative and didn't seem afraid of her. Then again, Marilynn appeared to out-and-out hate Nikki. It was a real tossup as to who she might let go first. If she had her way, it might even be the two of them. "Isn't it possible that one of us might get reassigned?"

"To another place in the store?" Marilynn appeared to consider this, but Nikki could tell any real consideration was fake. "I could look into it." She shot Nikki an evil grin. "There *might* be an opening in fragrance."

The rest of the day passed in a haze for Nikki. It was like she was operating on autopilot. The customers were fine and her work got done, but all her actions somehow seemed surreal. If she lost this job, she didn't know what she'd do. With her mom on the verge of losing her spot at the diner, that would leave Nikki's family practically destitute. Only Tony would be employed. And he just worked weekends and after school at the paper. He'd started as a gofer for them but had worked his way up to basic typing and data entry. He wanted to eventually be a reporter but knew he'd need a college degree to be taken seriously as a journalist. Meanwhile, they'd offered to keep him on after high school graduation. He could even work full time with benefits. But he'd never move up the ladder without that higher degree. His boss had been clear about that.

Nikki sighed, wondering what was to become of her. If only her aunt hadn't imposed those stupid conditions, everything would look different now. She'd be in for some money guaranteed to help her mom and baby brother. Plus, she could tell Marilynn to take this job and shove it. Nikki liked what she did and was skilled at it too, but she hated working for the department store. Especially since Marilynn had come along. Her dream was to open her own shop or even work freelance from home. She'd had enough people ask her if she did work on the side. Lots of folks in town needed help with hemming and simple adjustments. These were a breeze for her, but she knew there were people out there who couldn't even sew on a button. Even those who could often preferred to pay someone else to do the sewing. And plenty of people around here could afford that luxury.

Nikki felt like a pressure cooker with all sorts of heat and steam building up inside her. She had to find a way to get her hands on that inheritance. And she was running out of time. It was already the middle of January. She and Jack only had one month left to find her the perfect mate. Maybe Dean and Jeremy hadn't panned out, but there was always Kurt. Kurt was a good guy. Handsome and totally athletic. They'd also gotten along and had only broken up due to their conflict in schedules. He taught at a nearby private school and coached peewee-level ice hockey. Between his commitments and hers, they'd had trouble working out ways to see each other. Were he and Nikki to get together permanently, that problem would be solved. With some of Aunt Mallory's money, she could set up her own shop and establish more flexible hours. Plus, Kurt could afford to travel to all those historic places he taught about. Nikki could travel with him! Yeah, that would be fun. She'd liked Kurt. She really had.

Nikki reached into her purse and pulled out the small box that housed the necklace Jack had given her.

That was what she'd been missing: a good-luck charm.
She turned toward the mirror and snapped the catch at
the back of her neck. *Yes,* she thought studying her
reflection in the glass, *not too shabby.* She actually
looked datable when she smiled. Nikki thought of Kurt
and all the good times they'd shared. During the limited
times they'd been together… *Maybe this will work!*
Nikki thought hopefully. *Maybe I can really make it
happen after all.*

Chapter Seven

Nikki admonished Jack as they walked through the arena. "Did you really have to buy popcorn?"

"Why not?" He shoveled another handful into his mouth. "This is entertaining."

Nikki was wrong when she told her mom Jack had no disgusting habits. He ate nonstop, and at the most highly inappropriate moments. She didn't know how Angie could stand him, actually. He seemed to be growing more irritating by the day. As they approached the rink, he veered away from her.

"Where are you going?"

He motioned toward the stands with his popcorn bag. "Over there so I can get a good view."

A bunch of parents hunkered forward, their gazes intent on the actions of their offspring. Every few seconds, someone on the ice made a play, and the group erupted in shouts of encouragement or sounds of dismay.

"Ha-ha." She smirked.

"Best seat in the house." He flashed her a grin and strolled off. Before he got too far, he paused to glance over his shoulder. "Oh, and break a leg."

"This isn't acting, you know!"

He shrugged and shoved his hand in his popcorn, walking away.

Nikki fumed beneath her cream-colored sweater. She'd taken care to dress well in nice slacks and boots. One couldn't discount the impact of fashion when making a statement. Or more like a marriage plea. She'd planned the whole thing out and had decided to ease into it rather than springing the whole thing on Kurt up front. Besides, he was a little too occupied to reason through things now. She'd make arrangements to see him later, if he was game.

Nikki spied him by the bench, addressing a seated group of players. He'd stooped low to view them eye-to-eye and had temporarily removed his cap. He was broad across the shoulders with golden brown hair and a sturdy, masculine jaw. Nikki was struck by how attractive was, even now. He must have seen her coming, because he lifted his head in her direction and broke into a smile. It was a great smile too. Rock solid. Just like Kurt was a rock-solid guy. He said something to another coach, then waved her over. Nikki tried to keep from looking at the stands, but she snuck a peek anyway. Jack raised his popcorn bag in a mock toast. Infuriating. Really. She didn't know why she'd brought him along! Apart from the fact that he had a car and she didn't, which would have made it a tad more complicated for her to get here.

"Well, look at you!" Kurt stepped through the gate to give her a hug. "Gosh, Nikki. You look terrific."

"Thanks, you too." She smiled but felt a little twitch in her lips. She hoped he hadn't noticed.

He stared down at her with honey-brown eyes, and Nikki recalled why she once fell for him. He really was one hot man. Sweet too. "It was such a surprise to hear from you," he said as the game restarted behind him and commotion ensued on the ice. To his credit, he kept his eyes on her, even though he had every right to be distracted. "What made you call?"

"I...uh." She swallowed hard and gathered her nerve. "I've been thinking a lot about you."

His brow rose in a pleased expression. "Yeah?"

"Yeah. And here's the thing. I was wondering how you felt about—"

"What?"

A whistle squealed behind him, and this time, he looked.

"This probably isn't the best time."

He set his hands on his hips with a chuckle. "I am a little tied up, yeah."

"But later?" she asked with a hopeful lilt.

"Just what are you getting at, Nikki? And why the twenty questions on the phone about whether I was seeing anyone, or engaged, or"—he coughed into one hand—"married?"

She put on her best convincing mug. "We had some good times."

"Sure we did."

"Great times."

"I'd give them a B plus at least."

Her voice rose in shock. "B plus?"

"Just joshing." He grinned and shook his head.

"Coach!"

Kurt turned to see a scrap had broken out between two players on his team. His assistant was herding them into the penalty box and eyeing him with urgency. "I've got to run," he told Nikki.

"But later? Can we…?"

"Sure, sure. Love to catch up. Still got my number?"

She held up her cell in a yes.

"Great. Give me a buzz." Then he was off and onto the ice.

"That seemed to go well," Jack said when he rejoined her in the corridor. "At least I saw him smiling."

"Yeah. It was good." She slipped back into her coat, looking perplexed. "Real good. Went better than I thought. Way better than with the others."

"So?" Jack asked her. "Did you do it? Set up a date to discuss *your offer*?"

Her lips creased in a frown. "I wish you wouldn't put it like that."

Jack tossed his empty popcorn bag in a wastebasket and studied her. "What's wrong?"

"He said I was a B plus."

"B plus? What's that? Teacher talk?" In spite of himself, Jack chortled. "Hang on... He wasn't talking about in the sa—"

She wheeled on him. "What is it with you? Why are you always thinking dirty?"

"Me?" Jack had no clue what B plus meant, but— considering it came from Kurt—it couldn't be that bad. Nikki had always described him as a stand-up guy. In fact, he was likely the best candidate Nikki had.

"Yes, you!" Her tone was brittle. "This is nothing but a great big game for you, is it?" She stared him down with a fiery gaze, but there was moisture in her eyes.

"Hey," he said quietly. "I didn't even want *in* this game, remember? You dragged me along."

She raised a hand to wipe her cheek. "He said he'd go. Said he'd love to go out with me and catch up."

"That's...great?" Jack asked uncertainly.

"Not married. Not engaged. Not seeing anybody." She sniffed and pulled herself up a little straighter, but

Jack noted the fingers of her left hand rapidly drumming her thigh. "He might just be the one."

If Kurt was Nikki's Prince Charming, why did she look like she was going to break down in a bawling mess? Jack spoke carefully so as not to tip her over the edge. "So… Then…we'll just have to play this through. Take it step by step, right?"

She nodded, but she was crying, tears streaming down her face. When she spoke, it came out in a warble. "Right."

Jack held out his arms in a hug. "Come here."

She shook her head. "I can't."

"Why not?"

"I'll get mascara on your new parka."

"Oh for crying out… Forget that." He pulled her to him anyway, because he knew how badly she needed some comfort.

She let him hug her, then finally hugged him back. Hard, until it almost hurt.

"Plus," she said into his shoulder, "you smell like popcorn!"

Jack burst out laughing, then patted her back. "That's my Nikki," he said, stroking her hair. "And you know what, kiddo?"

She pulled back all bleary eyed to look at him.

"You're going to be all right."

She stopped crying and stared up at him. "I am, aren't I?"

"Of course you are. You're tough. Tougher than tough. Scary tough, even."

"I am?"

"You bet."

Her pretty blue eyes brightened. Then, oh no, something awful happened inside. It was like a tiny flutter, a subtle awakening, somewhere deep in his soul. *No!* Jack cursed it. *Go back to sleep!*

Nikki broke their embrace. "Did you say something?"

Fire torched Jack's nape. "Did I?"

"Are you tired, Jack?"

"What? No!"

"Well, no wonder! Must be exhausting." She playfully shoved his shoulder. "Being my best friend."

"It can get pretty taxing at times."

"Then come on. Drive me home." She linked her arm through his, apparently recovered. The only thing was Jack wasn't sure he had. Not completely. But he walked along with her anyway, like nothing at all had changed. Because it hadn't, really. Not as far as he could tell.

"Jack," she said when there were almost to his car, "I want to thank you for this. Thank you for everything."

The snow had stopped but was piled high in the parking lot. Big dirty mounds studded every row. But nothing could be murkier than the feeling in Jack's heart. The sooner she got this over with, the better. "No problem," he said, opening her door. "No problem at all."

A few mornings later, Jack rolled over in bed to nab his cell off the nightstand. It was just after seven, and he hadn't heard from Nikki since Saturday. Something was definitely up. He felt a hand on his shoulder, then heard Angie's groggy voice. "What time is it?"

"Still early, babe. Go back to sleep." He punched in Nikki's speed-dial number and scooted out of bed.

Angie wrapped the covers around herself with a yawn. "Who are you calling?" She was a sleepy mess, wavy auburn hair splayed out on the pillow. She was one of the best-looking women Jack had ever seen. Beautiful and good to him too. Jack would do well to remember that. "Come back to bed, baby."

"In a sec." He gave her a quick peck on her crown, then slipped out the door and shut it behind him. A few rings later, Nikki answered.

"Jack? Why are you calling so early?"

He walked to the living area and sat. "Why haven't you called?"

She hesitated just a moment too long. "I've been waiting on news to tell you."

"What news?"

"About me and Kurt."

"Have you seen him?"

"Not yet."

Jack eyed the calendar on the wall across the room. "Nikki, January's flying."

"I know it is, which is why I told him it's important."

"So what's the holdup, then?"

"Schedule conflicts."

Jack sighed heavily. "This is never going to work. Maybe we need to take a trip to Rhode Island."

"To see Peter? No."

"Yes. And this weekend. Pencil it in." He checked the day planner on the coffee table before him. "We'll have to leave super early on Sunday, but if you swap out your shift with Roger, maybe I can talk to my dad about coming in late."

"But I'm seeing Kurt on Wednesday."

"Wednesday?"

"It's my day off."

"Yeah, but not his."

"After school. I'm meeting him at The Home Run at four." Jack knew The Home Run was a sports bar and one of Kurt's favorite hangouts. Still, Wednesday seemed a long time away. That was practically another week.

"I don't see the harm in taking a road trip in the meantime."

"It's a waste of gas money. Peter's not my first choice."

Jack felt a lump in his throat. "Kurt is," he said quietly.

"Steady job, stable personality, secure… You can't blame me."

No, he couldn't blame her at all. The truth was Peter was a bit of a wildcard. At twenty-eight, he still had ambitions to make it big with his rock band. They had a manager now but were always on tour. What kind of promise did that hold? For Nikki? For a baby?

Of all Nikki's exes, Kurt really did make the most sense. So why did this feel wrong to Jack?

"I have a good feeling about this one. About Kurt, I mean. And I owe it all to you."

"Me?"

"Your eternity charm. It's working."

Jack hung his head. He could practically see her fingering the damn thing, the circular piece of jewelry dangling from the chain around her neck. "So you think you can have that with him? All of it?"

"I don't see why not. He's smart and certainly built." Jack had to give him that. The guy kept himself buff. "And the spirit thing? Well, we'll just have to take time to work on that."

"And being married will give you time."

"Exactly."

Jack didn't know why, but he suddenly felt down about the whole thing. What was more, he missed Nikki. "So when do you want to get together?"

"For what?" Her words shot like an arrow to his heart. She'd never asked him that before. Suggested he justify wanting to see her.

"To strategize."

"Thanks, Jack. But I've got this all sewn up."

"Okay, then," he said, drawing a breath. "I guess we'll talk after?"

"After would be great. I'll give you a call to let you know how it went."

"I think it would be better if we discussed it in person. Something this serious, Nikki? You're taking this final step."

"You're right," she said after a beat. "I'll drop by the restaurant later on Wednesday. Will around eight be all right?"

Jack felt like someone had filled his stomach with lead. He stared out the window and saw it had started snowing again. It pounded the glass with soggy streaks that matched the rain in his heart. This could really happen. Jack might actually lose Nikki. He wanted to wish her luck but knew he couldn't. Not this time. He spoke surely to cloak the emotion in his voice. "Eight will be fine. See you then."

Chapter Eight

When Nikki got to The Home Run at four, Kurt was already there, drinking a tall draft beer. She joined him at the bar and ordered coffee. She needed to keep her wits about her and play this whole thing right. Kurt raised an eyebrow when her java arrived. "Working later?"

"I left early. Roger spelled me."

Kurt sputtered a laugh. "I'd almost forgotten about Roger. How's he doing? Still giving Marilynn hell?"

"In his own quiet way."

"Well, good. She deserves it."

He paused in drinking his beer to study her. "You're looking good, Nikki. Really fine. Then again, you always were one fine-looking woman."

Nikki sipped from her coffee and grinned. "Still the same old Kurt."

"I'm not that old. At least not as old as that geezer you went with before me. What was his name? Justin?"

"Jeremy."

"Music conductor, that's right." He chuckled. "Wonder what he's up to now?"

Nikki's face warmed. "I wouldn't know."

"Probably after another young thing. Maybe two."

Nikki's flagged down the bartender and asked for some water. "How's your mom?" she asked, making small talk. "And your brother, Carl?"

"Both fine, thanks. How about your mom? And Tony?"

"Tony's good. He graduates this year."

"No way! I still remember him as peewee-size."

"Yeah well, he's man-size now. Nearly six feet."

"Whoa." Kurt pushed aside his beer and set his elbows on the bar. "What are his plans after high school?"

"Some of that's still getting worked out."

Kurt nodded, misunderstanding. "He's a kid. He'll find his way."

"Yeah."

"And your mom?"

"She's…not so well, to tell you the truth."

The lines around his eyes creased with concern. "What's wrong?"

"It's a neck thing, slipped disk."

"Ouch."

"Ouch is right, and she needs—" Nikki stopped suddenly to stare at him. "Kurt," she said abruptly, "how do you feel about marriage?"

"What?"

She folded her face in her hands, feeling like an idiot. *Great, Nikki. Just perfect. Wonderful proposal.*

Kurt lightly touched her shoulder, and she looked up. "Did I hear you right?" he whispered below the bar noise. "Did you just say something about marriage?"

She grimaced. "Sort of." Nikki heard a tap-tap-tapping sound, then realized it was her fingers drumming the bar. Kurt laid his hand over hers.

"Still doing that, huh?"

"Only sometimes," Nikki lied.

"Doll, what's going on? Are you in some kind of trouble?"

Nikki stared down at their hands as his overlapped hers. His touch was gentle, reassuring. She'd been right in remembering him as a really nice guy. "It's not trouble exactly," she told him. "More like a predicament."

His hand squeezed hers. "Why don't you tell me about it?"

"Do you remember me telling you about my Great-Aunt Mallory?"

"Mallory? No."

"I guess maybe I didn't. She'd been left pretty far in my past when I met you."

"But she came back?"

"No, she died."

"Geez, Nikki. I'm sorry."

"It's okay. I didn't really know her. So, apart from her being family and that part being sad… What I mean is, I didn't take it as hard as you think. I was just sorry for her at the end, about how she left things and how little she left behind."

"Poor woman. She was destitute?"

"Far from it. She was rich. Really rich, Kurt. Two million dollars rich."

"Wow. Guess her kids are set for a bit."

"She didn't have any kids. Only cows."

Kurt blinked in slow understanding. "Just what are you telling me, Nikki? That your aunt left you two million dollars?"

She met his gaze. "Under two conditions."

"What conditions?"

Nikki took a deep breath, then pushed ahead. "One, that I marry—"

"Oh, I get it." He pushed back to study her. Then suddenly he thumbed his chest. "Hold the phone!" he said, choking. "*You want to marry me?*"

People lined up and down the bar swiveled to stare at him. "Sorry!" He lowered his voice and turned to her. "Nikki, you can't be serious?"

Nikki's cheeks flamed. "I thought you'd at least be a little excited."

"Honey, this is nuts, and you know that."

"But I thought you…? I thought we…?" She felt on the verge of tears.

"Hey, hey," he said, patting her arm. "Don't do that. Don't cry, okay?"

"Okay." She pulled herself together, dabbing her face with a bar napkin. "I just didn't expect you to take it so hard."

Kurt's Adam's apple rose and fell. "I'm just in shock, doll. You can't blame me for that."

He was right; she really couldn't.

"So why did you pick me?" he asked. "Was no one else available?"

"What do you mean?"

"Nikki, you and I dated five years ago. It's been some time. I'm sure you had at least *one* boyfriend after."

Nikki didn't much see a way out of this. Honesty probably was the best policy. Especially since she intended to spend forever with the guy.

"He's married."

"I see."

Kurt downed the rest of his beer. "Two million smackers, huh?"

"It's only one million right up front. You'd get half."

Kurt whistled, then fell silent, fixated on the ball game on the TV overhead. Finally, he turned back to her. "No strings?"

"What do you mean?"

"About the money? Half a million is mine to do with as I please?"

"Sure."

"And all I have to do is marry you some time? Like after we've had a chance to get back together and make sure this is…?"

"It has to be by February fourteenth."

"Of this year?" He started choking again, coughing into the back of his hand. He grabbed her half-empty water glass and took a long swallow. "But why?"

"It was one of the conditions."

"Uh-oh, I almost forgot. You said there were two."

Nikki made a motion bringing her thumb to her index finger. "Yeah, but the second one's tiny."

"How tiny?"

"Oh…" She tried to recall what Tony weighed when he was born. "About eight pounds, two ounces, maybe?"

Kurt pursed his lips and avoided her gaze. After what seemed like forever, he finally spoke. "No can do, Nikki."

"It's for the second million," she told him. "You'd get another half. That would make you a mill—"

"You didn't hear me." When he stared at her, his expression was pained. "I said, I can't… Can't have kids."

Jack looked up from wiping down the counter as Nikki walked in the door. Since he was going to take over the business one day, he believed it important to understand all of its aspects. Whether that meant cashiering, serving a table, or ordering from a wholesaler, Jack was primed to fill in. While most of his time was dedicated to accounting matters, he made sure to spend at least a few shifts a week doing something else essential to running the restaurant. Tonight he was manning the bar.

She approached and tore off her scarf and hat. For some reason, she didn't look happy. She didn't seem disgruntled either. It was somewhere in between. More like preoccupied. He poured her a cold one and set it on the bar. "And?"

Nikki removed her mittens and coat before sitting. She was dressed in a pretty sweater, boots, and jeans. Jack noticed she was wearing the necklace he'd given her.

"Gosh, Jack." She met his eyes, but there was confusion in hers. "I don't know."

"What don't you know?"

"What to do about Kurt."

Jack feigned sympathy. "He shot you down, huh?"

"Actually." She picked up her beer and took a sip. "He accepted."

Jack signaled to another customer a few stools down that he was on his way. "He what?"

"He said yes."

Jack felt tightness in his throat and had trouble speaking past it. "Yes, that he'd marry you?"

She nodded, and Jack lifted a finger. "Hold that thought."

He hurried to refill the other customer's order, his head reeling. *Kurt said yes? That's not possible, is it? That this whole deal will come off? Nikki Constantino—my Nikki—is going to up and marry some other dude?* He stole a peek over his shoulder and caught her tapping her fingers again. She couldn't be happy about it. She just couldn't.

"You don't know how happy I am about this," she said when he returned. "I mean, seriously." She heaved a sighed for emphasis. "It's a huge relief!"

The room was bustling with the pre-weekend crowd, partially blocking Jack's view of the harbor. He could spy it just past her, lights twinkling along the edge of the dock through drifting snow. Perhaps the cold had gotten to her, or the winter air. Maybe if he gently coaxed it out of her, he'd learn the truth.

"Tell me what happened."

"It's a long story."

"Got no place to go but here."

"Bartender!" a customer called.

"And over there," he said with a grin. "Be right back."

This was wrong, all wrong, and Jack knew it. Kurt said yes? He wasn't supposed to do that. What happened to, *I'm sorry...* or *I'm happy being single...* or *Are you out of your mind?* Without even realizing it, Jack seemed to be moving on overdrive, doing everything twice as fast. People watched him wide eyed as he yanked back tap handles two-fisted, refilling two drafts at a time. "Two more local brews coming up!" He practically skated down the floor to set them at the edge of the bar. Honey-colored liquid sloshed beneath its frothy cap, nearly spilling over each mug's side. The woman looked at him askance, but the man took out his wallet. "Anything else?"

"That's got it, thanks," the guy said. "We'll just settle up."

By the time he got back to Nikki, her drink was a third of the way gone.

"You might want to slow down there."

"I'm only having one."

"Fine," he said, catching his breath. "What were you saying just then? Something about Kurt turning you down? I'm sor—"

"No! Jack, he said yes!" She narrowed her eyes in that accusatory way she did when she thought he wasn't listening.

"Oh, that's right," he said, tapping his fingers on the bar.

Nikki's mouth fell open. "Are you all right?"

"Fine. Just fine." He brought the offending hand to the back of his neck and rubbed his nape.

"O-kay…"

"So," he said, redirecting. "That's all great. Super terrific. Kurt said yes!" He pulled an empty glass from the rack and poured his own beer, holding it toward her. "Here's to you. To you and Kurt!"

"Are you supposed to be drinking?" Nikki whispered.

"Folks," he said a little more loudly. "I'd like to propose a toast to my friend Nikki. Soon to be married to her betrothed Kurt… What's his last name?" he asked her quietly.

She stared at him in disbelief. "Kenyon."

"Kenyon!" he proclaimed. "Here's to them both!"

Good tidings and cheers rang out throughout the room. Nikki laid her hand on his arm before he could take another drink. "What on earth are you doing?"

"Helping you celebrate," he replied evenly.

"Oh no, you don't." She snatched away his beer and set it aside.

"Hey!"

"Don't *hey* me. Give it to me straight, Jack. What's eating you?"

"Nothing. Why?"

"I just had the wild suspicion you might be upset about something."

"*I'm* upset because *you're* upset."

"Me?"

"Yes, you. If you're so hell-fire happy about marrying Kurt, why did you come in here looking like a kid who'd lost her…" Jack bit his tongue. He certainly wasn't going to say best friend. "Dog."

"That's a horrible thing to say."

"But it's the truth."

To his surprise, Nikki hung her head. After a few moments, she said, "Well, okay. You may have a point there."

"Ah-ha!"

"A very small point, but still…"

"Which brings me back to my original question."

"Which was?"

"What happened?"

"Oh that. Right." She pursed her lips a beat.

"Nikki…?"

"Okay, here's the deal. Kurt can't have kids."

Of all the things Jack was expecting, this wasn't one of them. "Can't or won't?" he asked gently.

"Can't. Sports injury when he was a teen."

"Ow." He involuntarily started to clutch himself but stopped short. "So, what's that mean? In relation to Mallory's will?"

"You know what that means. I wouldn't get the second million."

"Then that's a nonstarter."

"Not necessarily." She drew a breath and released it. "Look, I've been thinking this over all afternoon. Ever since I left The Home Run. Even took a long walk in the park."

"In this weather? No wonder it's hard for you to think."

"Actually, the fresh air helped clear my head. It helped me see that, in a totally unexpected way, Kurt's condition is a blessing."

"What?"

"Just, think about it, Jack. One million dollars is plenty. Heck, five-hundred thousand alone is more than enough. More than enough to help with my mom's operation…to help out Tony…to set up an at-home business for me and even put something away for retirement. Some sort of investment, a nest egg."

"So a baby is off the table?"

She met his gaze. "Don't you think it's better that way? What kid wants to be brought into the world as some sort of cash cow?"

"Nice choice of words."

"You know what I mean. It's simply not right. Plus, that puts added pressure on the marriage. There's so much to adjust to in the beginning anyway."

Just listen to her talking like this marriage is the most reasonable thing! It's only the baby part that's wrong. Right. He eyed her skeptically. "And Kurt's okay with this?"

"I haven't told him yet. I mean, I haven't told him I'm willing to go through with the wedding. I said that I'd think about it. Think about marrying him and forgoing meeting the second condition."

Jack ran his fingers through his hair. "Nikki—"

"Don't try to talk me out of it. You've already done that, remember? Next thing I knew, you were completely on board. Eager to help me find a husband. Well…" She smiled up at him. "Now it seems I have."

"Yeah," he said, still a little shell-shocked. "It seems that you have."

She handed him back his mug, then shared a dazzling smile. "Thanks for the good-luck charm. Looks like it worked."

Jack clinked his mug to hers. "Cheers," he said, totally not feeling it.

Chapter Nine

Emma stared at Nikki and blinked. "Tell that to me again, sweetheart. Who are you going to marry?"

"Kurt!"

"The school teacher?"

"That's the one."

"But, Nikki, you haven't seen him in years!"

Nikki fiddled with her scarf on the table. They were in her mom's kitchen, drinking coffee. It was Wednesday, her day off. "Oh yes, I have. Actually, it's really funny. We bumped into each other by accident and reconnected."

"When?"

"Um…" She rolled her eyes toward the kitchen clock, thinking. Tony would be home from school any minute. Then she'd have another set of questions to answer. That was, if she didn't get done with this fast. "Some time ago. Yeah, I think it was in October."

Emma studied her doubtfully. "October?"

"Yeah, I'm sure of it now. It was right around Halloween."

"Don't tell me," she said with a skeptical edge, "he came up to your door trick-or-treating."

"Don't be silly!" Nikki said with a laugh. "He came into the store for a suit."

Emma slowly sipped from her coffee. "And this was all before that little thing happened with Jack?"

"Oh yeah! Way before! Eons before!"

"And yet you opted to bring Jack here for New Year's Eve rather than your intended…"

"For heaven's sakes, Ma. Kurt wasn't my intended then! We've only just gotten engaged."

Her mom set an elbow on the table and rested her chin in her hand. "Somehow this all seems really sudden."

"Well, it is! Because that's Kurt! Ha-ha! A die-hard romantic!"

"So, he's flying you to Vegas for what? To get married by Elvis?"

"We'll find a real preacher, I'm sure."

"You'd better make sure. There are a lot of scam artists out there, I hear."

Nikki's fingers twitched on her coffee mug. She fought the urge to tap them. "We'll be fine. The arrangements are all taken care of." The truth was she still had to buy her airline ticket. Kurt already had his. He was headed out that way anyhow for a coaches' convention on the ninth. Why not make a trip of it and get hitched there, he asked? It was like multitasking! Nikki was a little let down he didn't want to make a separate plan just for them. But she understood the nature of their restrictions. They were under a timeline, and Vegas was a natural. Plenty of people to marry them there, and on very short notice.

"What about Jack?" her mom asked.

"What about him?"

"How does he feel about this?"

"He's fine with it. Really!"

"Hmm."

Her mom studied her face as if trying to read something.

"And Kurt, this old flame of yours… Does he kiss half as well as Jack?"

"Ma!"

Actually, Kurt hadn't tried to kiss her at all. Then again, she'd only seen him a few times lately. Once at the The Home Run, then later at a coffee shop where they'd worked out plans over a couple of Boston cream donuts. Naturally, Kurt had kissed her before. Way back when. She thought she remembered it as being good—real good. But the memory was a little murky. "That's a really inappropriate question."

"No. It's a motherly question. One that stems from genuine concern."

"About what?"

Emma met her eyes. "About the fact that maybe you're making a mistake. That maybe—just maybe—the guy who's meant for you has been right under your nose all along."

"I don't need to sit around and hear this," Nikki said, standing. "You're supposed to be happy for me."

"Happy about what?" Tony asked, walking in.

"Your sister's getting married," her mom said flatly.

Tony turned to her with pleased surprise. "To Jack?"

Jack clicked through the remote again then switched off the TV with a grumble. "Nothing decent's on."

Angie spoke from where she prepared homemade pizza by the stove. It was loaded with meats and cheeses, all the ingredients Nikki couldn't eat. "We've got over a hundred channels!"

"Yeah, and all of them are lame tonight." Jack had previewed lots of shows, but none of the details had registered. He couldn't believe it was already February eighth. So much had happened since Christmas Day, and very little of it was good.

"What makes you so grumpy tonight?"

"I'm not grumpy. Just hungry."

Angie smiled sympathetically. "Pizza will be ready in ten minutes." She slid it in the oven and poured them some wine. Jack hated that she was so nice to him. That only made his realization more difficult.

She joined him on the sofa and handed him a glass. "Let me see if I can cheer you up," she said, giving him a peck on the lips. Jack set down his wine.

"Angie…"

"What is it? What's wrong?"

He looked in her eyes, hating to break the news to her. "I can't…don't think that I can do this."

"Do what?"

"Keep pretending that everything's all right."

Her eyes misted slightly. "But it isn't?"

"You've got to believe me when I tell you, you've been the best." He took her hand. "The absolute best girlfriend a guy could want."

"Any guy except you?" she asked with hurt in her voice.

"I'm sorry. I can't get over—"

"Nikki," she finished for him. "Jack," she said gently. "She's marrying somebody else."

"I know that."

"Then why…?"

"I can't explain it. This just feels wrong. You and I…feel wrong."

"How long have you known?"

He spoke past the burn in his throat. "In some ways I guess I always have."

Angie hung her head. After a few quiet moments, it sounded like she was weeping. Jack released her hand, and she used it to wipe her cheek. "She doesn't want you, Jack," she said, looking up. "You know that."

But he didn't know that. Didn't know that at all. That might be what she'd said, but it wasn't what Jack believed in his heart. He'd convinced himself he didn't want Nikki either, but he'd been wrong. Categorically. He couldn't help but think perhaps Nikki had been mistaken too. There'd been something there when he'd kissed her, and in that motel room… Even at the arena, when she'd fallen into his arms. There was something more to their relationship now than mere friendship. Maybe there had been all along.

Jack stood and grabbed his coat. "I'm sorry. Really sorry about everything." The pizza timer went off as he reached the door. "But there's something I need to do."

Nikki opened her apartment door, stunned to see him. "Jack? What are you doing here?"

He strode into her small apartment and spied an open suitcase on the bed in the next room. "I came to tell you I think you're making a mistake."

"What?"

"Nikki, listen to me. You can't marry Kurt. That's crazy."

"All of this is crazy, Jack. You know that. But in its own crazy way, it also makes sense."

"But Vegas? You're going to *Vegas*, Nikki? Who's going to marry you? An Elvis impersonator?"

"Now you're sounding like my mom."

"I'll bet she thinks this is nuts too. Especially not knowing the details."

"She thinks it's a little sudden, yeah. But I explained to her I've always had a thing for Kurt. That I'd never really gotten over him."

"But you know that's not true."

"I... Hang on, Jack. Just what are you doing?"

He stepped toward her, and she inched back. "Trying to get you to think about this."

"I have thought about it."

"Not in the right way," he contested.

"There's something you don't know." She squared her shoulders and stared up at him. "I went to see your cousin Dave."

"The lawyer?"

"Yeah. And do you know what he told me?"

Jack shook his head, feeling like this had come out of left field. "No."

"He said it would take money—big money—to contest Aunt Mallory's will. Certainly a lot more money than I've got in the bank."

"I'll lend it to you."

"You can't do that. Your money's tied up in your dad's restaurant."

"I'll untie it, then. Take out a loan."

She met his gaze with urgency. "There isn't time."

He closed the distance between them. "Time is all we've got, Nikki. You and I both. We've got plenty, and without your Aunt Mallory's money. We can find a way to make it and to help your mom. Yes, and Tony too. We can do that." He paused and drew a breath. "Together."

Her words came out as a gasp. "What are you talking about?"

"Us, Nikki. You and me. We belong together. We always have. Don't you think there's a reason you've never kept a boyfriend, and no girl's ever worked out for me?"

"Maybe we're both relationship-challenged."

"Of course we are. Because we've been pursuing the wrong relationships. One of us is as guilty as the next."

"You can't mean that…? Jack! Just listen to yourself! What about Angie?"

"I broke up with her."

"You what? When?"

"Tonight." He took her in his arms, and this time she didn't resist. "I can't be with her when all I can think about is someone else." He dove into her eyes, his head and heart reeling. "Tell me you don't feel it. Tell me you've never felt anything between us and I'll walk away."

She stared up at him, blue eyes deep and soulful. It seemed an eternity before she finally spoke. "I'm marrying Kurt, Jack. The truth of the matter is I *do* need that money, and everything's been worked out." Although her words were harsh, her face softened with resolve.

He tightened his arms around her and pulled her close, so close it was impossible not to recall what his body felt like lying on top of hers. "Oh yeah?" he said, his mouth hovering over hers. "Then put this in your suitcase and pack it." Then he kissed her hard, bringing his lips to hers with all the ardor he'd bottled up for a decade. She sighed into his kiss, accepting it willingly, her tongue tangling with his, igniting a fiery passion in his soul. This was *his Nikki*, utterly and completely. Mind, body, and spirit: all three. He broke their embrace, leaving her breathless, and zipped up his coat.

Her hair was disheveled, her lips deep red. "Where are you going?" she asked, looking dazed.

"Away."

"Away?" she asked weakly.

"You have twenty-four hours to think about it. Then I'm not doing this anymore. It's all in or nothing, Nikki. If you get on that plane to Vegas, you and I are through."

Chapter Ten

Nikki walked toward the sofa on wobbly knees, holding on to furniture for support as she went. What just happened, and how had she suddenly lost all sense of reason? The truth was it was hard to think about anything at all besides being wrapped up in Jack's kiss. He'd totally blown her socks off, and nearly the rest of her clothing too. She'd never known she could experience that kind of passion with Jack, although a little voice in her soul said this was something she'd always suspected. Year after year, she'd fought her attraction to him, telling herself she was mistaking friendship for desire. She loved Jack. She always had. But in a way that was more about the two of them being buddies, right? Nikki sank down on the fluffy cushion, her heart careening wildly out of control. Jack! *Her Jack* had turned out to be a powerhouse kisser, and—okay, so she'd admit it—one incredibly sexy, desirable man. Plus, he desired her. That much was clear. While he'd hinted at that forever, he'd never so completely shown it until now. And wow, had he shown it. Full force.

Nikki stretched out her left hand and surveyed her empty finger. In another couple of days, a man was going to put a ring upon it. But was Kurt really the right man? Nikki tried to imagine herself being married to Kurt. Really imagine. She saw a future of peewee games and late nights of him grading school papers while she did her stitching. It would be a comfortable, practical existence. Fine for a stable future, and a partnership between… Nikki sat up with a start, slammed by the realization. It wasn't Jack she thought of as a friend, but Kurt! When she thought of her and Jack being married, she saw...roses and champagne and rumpled sheets in hotel rooms, and heavens! Babies! More than one, with dark wavy hair and Jack's gorgeous brown eyes. She recalled the feel of his body pressing hers and the fire of his kiss, and knew she longed for more of him. What they'd had together hadn't been enough. It could never be enough. She was glad Jack had broken up with Angie. She couldn't bear to think of him with her or any other woman. Not having the knowledge that he could be all hers. And— Nikki swallowed hard—understanding that she wanted him to be. Nikki stared in a sweat at the suitcase in the next room. She had to do something about her arrangements with Kurt, and soon. She checked the clock. It was nearly eleven. She couldn't go see him tonight. Kurt had a plane to catch in the morning. She'd head over there first thing.

When Nikki got out of bed, the sun was streaming through the window. The snow had let up, and the sky was a brilliant blue. She showered and stepped into her clothes, her heart bounding. For once in her life, she didn't feel nervous. Nikki knew precisely what she had to do. Jack was right about everything. Dean nailed it too. It was impossible for Nikki to fall for another guy as long as Jack was in the picture. And she wanted him there, all in. Nikki wasn't just attracted to Jack, she loved him. As in, *Love* with a capital L. The sort that went way beyond friendship and shot her straight up to the moon. Nikki set down her coffee and did a little pirouette around her apartment. "Wheeee!" *So this is what it feels like? It's like floating...or flying...or—*

Bonk! Nikki called herself up short and rubbed her head. She'd just danced clear into the refrigerator. "I'm a hazard to myself!" she yelped with a happy laugh. *And boy, doesn't it feel good!*

Thirty minutes later, Nikki stepped off the bus and headed up the steps of Kurt's apartment building. He met her coming out the door with his suitcase in tow. "Nikki!" he said in surprise. "I was just on my way to pick you up."

She stopped him as his feet met the slush on the brick step. "Do you mind?" She lightly patted her lips in an invitation to a kiss.

Kurt glanced at the passersby busily bustling down the street. "What? Here?"

She nodded and pushed him back toward the landing. He backed up a step and took her in his arms. "Well, all right. But just a quick one. We wouldn't want to miss our—" He gazed past her shoulder. "Wait. Where's your suitcase?"

While she felt sure in her heart, Nikki wanted to be one hundred percent certain in her body too. She'd lied to her mom about Kurt. The truth was, back in the day, his kiss had rocked her world. Before he could stop her, she wrapped her arms around his neck and planted one firmly on his lips. Hmm. They were there. Warm and all. But sizzling? Jack Hudson-hot? *Not.*

"What was that for?"

She licked her lips, then told him primly, "Just checking."

"Checking what?"

Nikki looked up and saw the sun had darted behind some dark clouds. Light flurries suddenly dotted the air. "Kurt," she said solemnly. "I have something to tell you."

He cocked his head to the side.

"I'm not going to Las Vegas."

"But what about the—"

"It's not you. It's me."

"Well, yes. I guessed that. Nikki, has something happened?"

"Yeah. I've learned that love can't be bought."

"Hang on a second. I never said the L word."

"Didn't have to. I'm planning to say it to someone else."

He studied her a beat. "Is this about Jack?"

Nikki glanced down at her chest to see if she was wearing a sign. Then she recalled that, in a manner, she was. That beautiful necklace Jack had given her. Though it was underneath her coat so Kurt couldn't see it. It was hard to say it, but Nikki knew she had to tell him the truth. "I'm so sorry, Kurt. I guess it's always been about Jack."

He floored her by breaking into a grin. "You and he will make some mighty fine babies."

"What?"

"I'm just saying, Nikki. I've seen that one coming for a very long time. Honestly, I was stunned you didn't ask him first."

"You're not…mad about this?"

"To be honest, I was having second thoughts myself."

"You were?"

"It's hard to marry a girl who's hung up on somebody else. No matter how great she is."

A taxi pulled up to the curb. "That's my ride."

"Thanks for being so understanding, Kurt. I wish there was something I could—"

"There is." His eyes twinkled. "If you ever come into that cash, do me a favor and throw a few dollars in the direction of my school."

"But it's private. The board's got tons of money."

"Yeah, but there are kids who should go there who can't afford it. Boys on my team who could really change their futures given that sort of chance. I was going to set up a scholarship fund with some of that money. I mean, once I had it."

Her heart melted. She'd been so right about Kurt. He really was terrific. His goal was worthy too. If Nikki ever found herself in a position to help with that, she wanted to. "I promise," she told him. "I'll do that."

Nikki's next move was finding Jack, but he sure didn't make it easy. She went to his apartment, but his car was missing. She checked at the restaurant, but his dad said he'd gone down to the docks to speak with their fish supplier. Nikki fitted her knit hat more firmly on her head as she followed the wooden walkway toward the marina. The snow was coming down harder now, pounding in heavy wet flakes. She wasn't even to the end of the slip when she saw him approaching. He strode toward her, repressing a smile.

"Don't you have a plane to catch?"

She sighed, surveying his handsome face. "Not anymore."

Snow dusted his dark cap, and in that instant, Nikki had a glimpse of how Jack might look at eighty. She knew without a doubt she'd love him just as much then.

The wind whipped up around them, howling off the water. "Nikki?"

"I was just thinking about how great you're going to look old."

"Thanks, I think."

"And I want to be there, Jack."

"What?"

"All in. Every step of the way."

She grabbed his hand and dropped down on her knees. Geez, the dock was frigid!

"Kiddo?" He stared down at her in shock. "You're going to get frostbite."

"Yeah? Well, I don't care." She tugged at his hand, holding his worn leather glove in both her mittens. "Because here's the thing, Jack Hudson. I may be a bit of a ditz when it comes to some things, but with others, I'm crystal clear. I mean, a little slow on the uptake, maybe… And I know sometimes my emotions get the best of me…"

"Only sometimes," he agreed.

"But, Jack—"

Man, he was gorgeous. The most impossibly hot guy she'd ever seen. How on earth did it take her so long to notice?

"You're the most wonderful guy I've ever met. Thoughtful, genuine, kind. And you kiss like a house on fire!"

Jack's eyes widened.

"Which is why I know you're right. You and I were destined to be. Mind, body, and spirit. All those connections rolled into one. I've felt it for a long time, only I didn't understand it. Didn't know what it was, because I couldn't give it a name."

"But you can now?" he asked, staring down at her. There was warmth in his heady dark eyes. Warmth and encouragement too. "Say it, Nikki. I need to hear those words."

She tried to speak forcefully, but her voice fell apart, cracking up as her eyes brimmed with tears. "I love you, Jack. I love you so much. Please forgive me for taking so long."

He tried to pull her up and into his arms, but she stopped him.

"Wait. I have something important to ask you. And, this has nothing to do with Mallory's money."

His brow rose in expectation.

"Will you marry me, Jack? Marry me and have my babies?"

"Did you say babies?" he asked in wonder. "With an S?"

She nodded as tears streamed from her eyes.

He yanked her up on her feet then, and into to his arms. "You crazy, marvelous woman, I love you back."

Hope welled in her heart. "Does that mean yes?"

"Baby," he said with a grin. "You bet!"

Then he kissed her so fiercely that Nikki's knees went weak, and the snow melted away as if they were in a dream.

Five days later, they were kissing again, this time before the neighboring county's sheriff. Jack's dad called in some favors and helped arrange a quickie ceremony. He, Emma, and Tony all stood by as witnesses. After breaking the happy news to her mom about this wedding, Nikki fessed up about Aunt Mallory. Since she and Jack were determined to be together anyway, they couldn't see the point in tossing away a million bucks. They'd worry about the second million when the time came, though they weren't going to let that rush them starting a family.

Between Jack's business and Nikki's new job, they'd be more than set with the first part of her inheritance. And that would be after helping with Emma's operation and buying Tony a community college tuition plan. Her brother was super excited and eager to study hard so he could earn his way into a nameplate university. He hoped to transfer on a scholarship, or else work part-time and take out loans to fund the rest of his way. Nikki and Jack were being generous enough in getting him started.

Nikki smiled happily around the room at her warm, loving family. They'd all meant so much to her, and now she finally had a way to give something back. Jack did too. His dad would get to retire early, and both he and Nikki had agreed to set a little money aside for Kurt's worthy scholarship fund. Life was all coming together in such a wonderful way. What was more, today was a day meant for love. It was February the fourteenth.

Jack shook the sheriff's hand, thanking him for his time, and the official shared an informed look. "As a newly married man," the sheriff said, "I just want you to remember one thing." Since he was the guy with the gun, Jack wasn't prepared to argue. Besides, he was out-of-this world happy. So thrilled that Nikki had become his bride.

"Yes, sir?"

"Marriage being what it is these days, it can sometimes be marred by rocky waters. Little life events that can stir things up or slow a relationship down. But as long as you remember three little words, you'll always get through your travels. Smooth sailing."

Jack didn't have to guess. He thought he knew, but the sheriff surprised him. "Nikki," he said with a grin. "You're right!"

The room burst into laughter as his dad slapped his back. "Wise words, young man."

"Yeah," Nikki said, nudging him. "Better not forget them."

Her eyes were a beautiful blue, her hair dark and lovely and piled up in waves as she wore that pretty white gown. They wouldn't have a traditional honeymoon but would fly to the Midwest with their paperwork first—to ensure the farm was well taken care of and Big Mama and her fellow cows too. Later, when Jack's restaurant shut down for a week in March, he was whisking her off to the Bahamas. His treat. It would be hard to treat her as easily once she was fully loaded, so he planned to take advantage now. "I'll never forget how right you were about something very important."

"Yeah?" she teased. "What's that?"

"Asking me to be your groom." He started to kiss her again, but Tony stopped him with a whisper.

"Maybe you guys should get a room."

"That's right!" Jack's said brightly. "I already booked one."

He slipped into his coat and helped Nikki with hers.

She arched an eyebrow, and his heart skipped a beat. "Did you now? Where?"

"Uh-huh, it's a surprise." He bent low and scooped her into his arms, and Nikki squealed.

"Jack! You're supposed to carry me over the threshold! But not here!"

"I'm practicing up," he said with a smile. Then he carted her out of the courthouse and through the snow as the others stood on the steps and waved good-bye. Jack was never going to forget this day, not as long as he lived. And the beautiful thing was, every single one of those days would be spent with his very best friend.

Epilogue

Emma extended her arms toward the cherubic baby. "Come on, sweetheart. Bring Big Mama to Grandma."

The little girl with raven curls clutched her stuffed cow with a happy coo and toddled over. Only last week, she'd taken her first steps, and Nikki had been here to see them, thanks in large part to her having a job that enabled her to work at home.

"She's doing all right," Jack said proudly.

"More than all right," Tony added. "She'll be running track soon."

Nikki laughed, her spirits light. "Let's not rush her."

Cutout paper hearts adorned their apartment along with cupid decorations Nikki found at the craft store. It was Valentine's Day, and their baby had just turned one-year-old at Christmas. While she and Jack had intended to wait and carefully orchestrate starting a family, life had other plans. Their birth control failed them in the Bahamas, though that was scarcely any wonder considering all the activity they'd undertaken. Nikki was caught off guard, but Jack called it karma. Something totally meant to be: their destiny.

Looking at her daughter now Nikki knew with her whole heart that Jack was right.

Emma set the child on her knee and gave her a kiss. "I still can't believe you named her Mallory."

"Mallory's the one who brought us together," Jack explained.

In its own strange way, it was true. "Plus," Nikki said, "she didn't really leave anyone behind. Any sort of legacy."

Emma smiled warmly at Nikki. "Oh yes, she did."

Jack brought his arm around Nikki in a hug, and the charm dangling from her neck shifted. In the past year, she'd removed the necklace only once—and that was due to hospital regulations. The eternity charm had worked like a dream, and this was one dream Nikki never wanted to wake up from.

"You two look good together," Emma said. "Good and happy."

"Yeah," Jack quipped with a grin. "I'm going to love her till the cows come home."

"What's that mean?" Tony wondered.

Nikki looked up at her husband and smiled. "For a *very* long time."

After Emma and Tony left and they'd put Mallory down for her nap, Jack pulled Nikki onto his lap on the sofa. "Come here, you," he said, nuzzling her neck. "I need some mommy time."

"You really like being a daddy, don't you?"

"Aw man, I love it. That's *Love* will a capital L… Nikki? Why are you looking at me that way?"

Her cheeks warmed in spite of herself. "I think we better investigate a different method of birth control."

"What?" His face lit up. "You can't mean…"

Nikki nodded, her whole world gone fuzzy. She couldn't believe it, but it was true. She'd taken the test this morning. Three times. Little Mallory was going to have a baby brother or sister.

"Holy cow! That's terrific!"

He kissed her hard on the lips, and her heart beat wildly.

"You're not upset?" she asked him. "It's not too soon?"

"I guess it's fate." He was still in awe. "Karma!"

"I thought it was fertility."

Jack chuckled and laid her down beneath him. "Hmm. That too."

"Jack! What are you doing?"

"As long as we're all in anyway…" She felt the taut muscles in his chest, the rock-hard press of his thighs. Current tore down her spine, then sparked to other regions.

"Here?"

"Oh my sweet baby, I'd have you anywhere at all. Just say you'll be mine."

"Always," she breathed as his mouth closed in.

The End

A Note from the Author

Thanks for reading *Baby, Be Mine*. I hope you enjoyed it. If you did, please help other people find this book.

1. This book is lendable, so loan it to a friend who you think might like it so that she (or he) can discover me, too.

2. Help other people find this book: write a review.

3. Sign up for my newsletter so that that you can learn about the next book as soon as it's available. Write to GinnyBairdRomance@gmail.com with "newsletter" in the subject heading.

4. Come like my Facebook page: http://www.facebook.com/GinnyBairdRomance.

5. Comment on my blog: The Story Behind the Story at http://www.goodreads.com.

6. Visit my website: http://www.ginnybairdromance.com for details on other books available at multiple outlets now.